MISS FITZ'S CLASSROOM OF ARCANE MAGICS

KEVIN A DAVIS

Inkd
Publishing

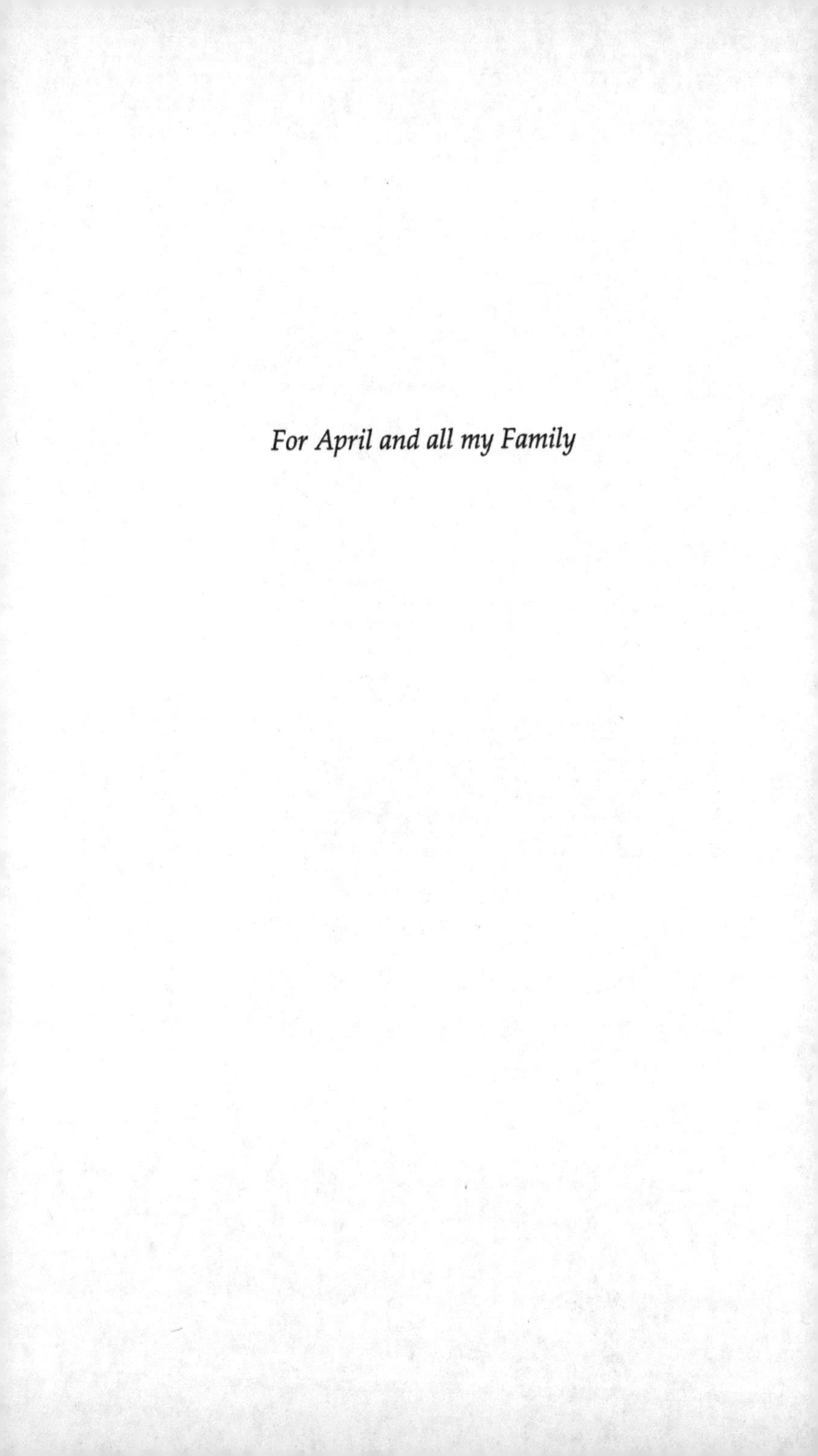
For April and all my Family

MISS FITZ'S CLASSROOM OF ARCANE MAGICS

CONTENTS

INTRODUCTION

Tommy Williams is an average witch about to encounter some very unusual circumstances. His classmates, Serena and James, will be by his side for most of the adventure, but there are some things Tommy must learn for himself.

The portals to Miss Fitz's classroom are at the library in Monticello, Florida, but you won't be able to get through unless she lets you.

CHAPTER 1
DANGEROUS

I'M TOMMY WILLIAMS, just an average thirteen-year-old boy. Average in height, average in weight. Grades — average. As a witch — just average too. People sometimes forget I was there at all.

That's why when Miss Fitz, my teacher in advanced magics, visited my mom and dad after the last day of mundane sixth grade, on Thursday afternoon, they didn't remember I was upstairs reading in my room I'd come home at noon, plugged in my cell phone to charge, and started a reread of *Skyward*.

I had heard them answer the door and assumed it was one of Mom's friends. It took until Miss Fitz let out a harrumph that I recognized her voice from the kitchen on the first floor.

Okay, one thing I'm not average about is being able to sneak down the stairs and not let the fourth step from the bottom squeak. The living room had afternoon light splashing over our tan sofa and reflected off the black flat-screen television. I gripped the smooth white railing as I paused, tilting my head to listen.

Miss Fitz's voice had a distinctive scratchiness to it. Like my aunt who smoked cigarettes. "Trust me. It's the only way he'll ever get his second sight, if he has the propensity."

"It's dangerous." My dad sounded nervous.

"I'll be there to make sure they're safe." Miss Fitz sounded as rough with him as she did when we were in her classroom.

When they grew silent, my eyes flicked toward the kitchen and I tensed, unsure if they had heard me.

"Very well. I did wonder when he turned thirteen and nothing came of it. That's not a skill readily passed down. He might not even have second sight." So Mom agreed with Miss Fitz, and whatever was dangerous had to do with me.

My friend Serena would have barged in on their meeting and demanded to know what they were talking about. Our friend James probably had his house wired for sound so he would have heard the whole conversation. I just stood there blinking until a chair scraped on the kitchen floor sending me sneaking back up the steps.

I recognized Miss Fitz's quick footsteps heading for the living room. A quick glance up the stairs told me I'd never be out of sight in time. Standing straight, I thudded onto a lower step and began climbing down to meet them. Maybe they'd just say, "Oh, Tommy, we were just talking about you and something dangerous. Sit and let us tell you about it."

Instead, Miss Fitz rounded the corner and squinted at me suspiciously through round glasses. "Tommy." She addressed me with a flat tone.

"You're home, dear." Mom sounded surprised as she entered the living room. She tugged at her cream-colored blouse.

"That he is," said white-haired Miss Fitz. She touched one of the carved ornaments on the necklace that hung down her black turtleneck. She gave one hard squint and spun for the front door. "Don't be late for class tomorrow."

"Yes, Miss Fitz." I stood awkwardly, wanting to blurt out a question about what kind of danger I was in, but didn't. Otherwise, I'd have to admit I was eavesdropping on their conversation. Unlike regular school, her classes lasted all year.

"We were just talking about the summer curriculum," Dad said. I'd wondered why he was home early from the insurance office, still dressed in his blue button-down shirt. He moved to follow Miss Fitz to the door.

"That's right, dear. She's working on the details now. Are you hungry?" Mom rested her hand on my shoulder and I straightened. She was a much better witch than Dad and might have some trick up her sleeve to catch me lying, spying, or prying. They obviously weren't going to tell me plainly what was going on; parents seldom did.

I blurted out the first thing to come to mind. "Doritos."

"I'll make you a sandwich." She held me in place with a firm grip. "Good evening, Miss Fitz. Thank you."

Dad's lips twitched, then he nodded. "Yes, thank you. Let me see you out."

Mom nudged me toward the kitchen, as I glanced back at Miss Fitz standing in the doorway. I felt a chill up my neck at her hard stare that told me she guessed that I'd listened in. She had magic up her sleeves, in her socks, and hidden in her curly white hair.

Mom chatted on about our upcoming family trip to Nantucket where most of her witch family lived. However, she didn't mention the visit by Miss Fitz, or anything dangerous in my future. *Why not? Too dangerous? Would it mess up whatever they expected me to learn?* I wrestled with asking her, but that would expose my eavesdropping. Instead, I nodded while she made a sensible, average sandwich on white bread. I did get a small portion of Doritos with it. Dad disappeared, since he was the worst liar in the house.

"Your grades will be out soon." Mom took a seat at the table while I ate.

"I don't think I did well in math."

"You placed average in the assessment test." She flashed a quick smile.

My mom was anything but average. She ran a business downtown, had all kinds of degrees, and wrote stories for books and magazines. Her hair was brown like Dad's and mine, but it had a fancy look to it. *Did I disappoint her?*

I'd prefer not to be average. I'd rather be Amelia Earhart, Spensa, or Indiana Jones. I dreamed of being a pilot, though I'd rather be the old-fashioned kind with goggles. Maybe an astronaut or an archaeologist digging up forgotten cities. Because of that, I didn't mind that Miss Fitz had something dangerous in mind for me. In fact, the more I thought about it the more I daydreamed about a magical adventure with an irate Yeti.

CHAPTER 2
MISS FITZ'S CLASSROOM

MIDMORNING THE NEXT DAY, I arrived at the Jefferson County R.J. Bailar Public Library on Water Street. James's electric bike was locked on a pole in front with a silicone coated cable while Serena's ancient bike with scratched red paint had a cheaper lock with what looked like a wire compared to his.

I skidded off my bicycle and positioned it against a farther pole. Serena was usually the late one. We'd been plotting last night how to get Miss Fitz to give me more details. Obviously, Serena had been even more anxious than me to get the scoop on what was planned. I stuffed my helmet in my backpack and whipped the cable around my bike.

When I raced for the door to the library and yanked it open, I slid to a stop. Just inside the opening, two older women stood facing each other chatting in the doorway to my left. They barely gave me a glance.

Including the one the ladies blocked, there were three rarely used rooms that stretched down the left side of the hall to the back exit; the last was our portal that led to Miss Fitz's classroom.

I swallowed, nodded, and turned right into the main part of the building. James read a book at the new arrivals section, watching for the women to move out of sight of the portal. It wouldn't work if someone could see us.

James was a werebear with brown skin, black curly hair, and a love of all things robotic or tech. He was also my oldest and closest friend. He flashed an annoyed smile as I approached.

The librarian at the counter gave a pleasant nod and continued working at his monitor. An older man sat in one of the chairs reading while a woman in sporty clothing drifted up and down the aisles.

I picked up a YA novel, flipping pages as if scanning it. "Hey. I tried to call you."

His eyes flicked to the women near our portal. "Yeah. I missed it. Saw it when I packed for the ride here. I'm working on a bot for a game."

I shrugged and swapped for a book with a dragon's head on it, not that the librarians cared. "It was a long message."

"*Your* parents would allow you to do something risky. Mine wouldn't. They're paranoid." He frowned. "You thought me and Serena might be part of this dangerous test? Miss Fitz hasn't been by my house. I would have picked it up on the cameras."

"Miss Fitz said, 'they're' so I assumed you two.

Gods I hope she didn't mean the older class." I cringed at the idea of having to work with Chet; I could deal with Vic or Piper. "I tried to get them to say more at dinner, but Mom changed the subject."

He didn't appear worried about it, but he was right. I couldn't imagine his parents allowing him to be in danger. "You bring everything?" he asked.

I patted the strap to my backpack. "I wouldn't forget." We had plans for the tree house this afternoon. I *had* almost forgotten, worrying about Miss Fitz's visit.

He shoved the book back on the rack. The two women had stepped inside the room, closing the door behind them. I put the dragon story on its shelf and led the way toward the entry hall.

The last door was marked "Genealogy" and almost no one went in there. There was a camera above the door by the back exit, but Miss Fitz told us not to worry about it.

James glanced around us, checking if we were visible to anyone.

The portal wouldn't work if someone could see us, so I didn't worry as I reached for the surface. The door softened to the consistency of mud under my fingertips, then sucked me into it with the usual snap. The rush of movement felt exaggerated as blackness flickered around me, before the faint light of the classroom met my eyes. I stepped automatically, moving much slower than the sensation suggested, and the wire grate of the stairs rang with my landing. Below me, Miss Fitz peered up from her desk on the left side of her long classroom.

The room stretched sixty or more feet from the stairs to the dark Neverdoor at the far end. The walls were polished rock, though wood shelves climbed up most of them. A stone floor had carpets in some areas; a blue and silver rug stretched at the foot of the winding stairs.

Tan-skinned Serena stood in front of Miss Fitz, in the midst of an obvious conversation. Serena called her short brown hair auburn and wore a black tank top, jean shorts, and those monster shoes she liked. The mundane teachers wouldn't let her wear combat boots in regular school, but it was technically summer. She turned up and flashed a grin at us as James joined me.

We started down the spiral staircase.

"We will be going on a field trip!" Serena sounded ecstatic, probably because we'd been theorizing about the possible dangers over messages last night. She wanted to use her sword skills.

I dashed down the steps. "Oh, cool, where?"

Miss Fitz's gravelly voice sounded more annoyed than usual. "This summer is all you need to know. You're too quick to presume." She settled her stare on Serena. "All of you. Focus on your lessons."

A chuckle in the back brought my attention to a deeper section of the classroom where Miss Fitz's alchemy lab took up a space before the practice area. The older students, Piper, Vic, and unfortunately, Chet were huddled there at a table filled with bottles from an experiment. It was best to ignore them, except for Vic. If he was alone, we could talk.

"I hadn't presumed anything," I lied. "Just curious. We've got a *lot* planned for the summer." We did. We'd worked out upgrades to our cloaked tree house in the woods behind Serena's house. James had a plan to get a wind turbine hooked up for electricity so we could play games and not drain our batteries. That was at the top of our list. The cloaking magic would have to be altered.

Miss Fitz let out a distrustful harrumph. With a jingle of her brass charm bracelet, she pointed to the closest section of her classroom with tables and a white board where we'd start class today. Among the many odd animal shapes dangling from her wrist, there was a bell we only heard when she wanted to emphasize a point.

We'd have a continuation of lessons on shield magic that didn't involve using a focal, like my staff. The class had been going on for two weeks and she still hadn't let us try the spells.

The three of us headed for our seats, Serena bouncing excitedly most of the way. "I hope I get to bring my sword."

If the "field trip" was the danger Miss Fitz had warned my parents about, at least I wouldn't be with the older witches. Chet did everything he could to make my life miserable.

Miss Fitz followed us quickly, her steps heavy on the carpet. "Enis Rey Polis is the beginning of which incantation?"

We hadn't even grabbed our notebooks off the back shelf yet, but James answered without a pause. "A full sphere shield. Difficult if surrounding more than yourself."

"Correct, James." She moved to her place at the whiteboard and drew a four-line sigil as we scrambled to get pens and notebooks. "Tommy, how does this relate to that spell?"

I pushed my flight goggles off my notebook to grab the pad along with a pen. "It will enhance the incantation, strengthening the shield."

"If, Serena?"

"Uh." Serena hesitated, shifting in her seat and flipping pages. "It's got to be inside the bubble, right?"

"Question or answer?" Miss Fitz frowned steadily at my friend.

"Uh, answer?"

Miss Fitz blinked in her slow disapproving way. "Very well. Why is that difficult?"

Swallowing, Serena carefully did not glance at James who would know the answer. "I guess you'd need something to write on."

"Correct." Miss Fitz never smiled, but she softened when she turned to her star pupil, James. He was smart enough that he could have taken the tests to move up to mundane High School this year, but he'd stayed with us. "What modern day solutions would *you* suggest, James?"

"A pen." I was surprised at his simple answer,

coming from someone who could build a drone out of scrap parts. "You could write it on your skin."

"Very good. Now we'll start reciting the incantation, focus on inflection."

We spent the next half an hour repeating words more ancient than Latin. Serena, the most gifted in magic, was the worst at getting close to Miss Fitz's expectations. James was easily the best since he remembered everything she taught. I was in the middle. *Average.*

In the meantime, Chet and the older students finished up their lesson, and while Vic handed Miss Fitz a bottle filled with thick, green liquid, Chet and Piper passed too close behind me. That's when the smell started. Something between rotting eggs and burnt steak wafted around me. I grimaced and spun to watch Chet strolling toward the stairs, looking over his shoulder with a grin so wide I knew he'd done something. Without thinking, I rubbed the back of my head, smearing a wet, gray gob onto my palm. The stench grew and I gagged, nearly puking.

"Contain yourself, Tommy." Miss Fitz chided as she inspected the older student's resulting bottle, sniffing it with a satisfied nod to Vic. "Very good. Three days off."

Vic gave me a quick apologetic smile as he joined the rest of the older class who let out a quick cheer and raced up the stairs.

"Permission to use the head, Miss Fitz." I held up my palm to show the inky dark smudge that reeked.

Serena and James were leaning away from me with winces.

"Be quick about it."

Careful not to touch anything with that hand, I pushed back from the table, jumped up, and ran for the thin door between the classroom section and the lab. She called her bathroom a "head," though we weren't on a ship. I didn't think so anyway. We'd asked, but she hadn't answered. Our best guess presumed that her classroom sat under the library and both portals. The walls, ceiling, and floor were rock after all. The after-hours portal we used during the library's closed hours was attached to the back wall of the building.

Inside the head, the small cubicle carved in rougher stone than the classroom, had a metal toilet, a stubby faucet, and a basin the size of one side of my kitchen sink. Water didn't help get rid of the stench. I washed most of the goo off my hand with a heavy dose of soap, but I couldn't get it out of my hair and the smell got worse in the small confines. "Jerk." All of the older class would have known about the prank, even Vic; he stuck up for me when he could.

Is there a spell for removing a retch-inducing stench?

Miss Fitz gave me a quick glower for taking so long as she ended the spell lesson with a flourish that sent my notebook and pen floating back to the shelf behind our chairs. James and Serena were already putting theirs away. "Tincture of houndstongue today. Serena, extra care."

Still reeking, I joined the others while Serena held

her hands close with her lips pursed. She could toss one of the older kids onto their backs with her martial arts, and had, but alchemy frightened her. She'd failed enough experiments that caution made sense.

Getting her mind off it was easy. "What will we need to prepare for our field trip, Miss Fitz?"

Serena's eyes glittered.

"No poking about, Tommy. You'll know everything you need to when the time comes. Focus"

The alchemy lab had three black stone tables with a polish that shone; the largest rested in the center of the space while the smallest held a sink. Shelves lined both walls. One side contained raw ingredients in jars, baskets, and cloth bags, while the opposite side was finished potions in bottles or boxes. The older boys had cleaned up all but a folded shred of paper and an empty jar. James picked up both to clear our space.

A blue cloud burst from the paper as he lifted it, dousing his tight curls and arm. He blinked and froze, but none had gotten in his eyes.

"Chet," I growled.

"Elderfitch. Harmless." Miss Fitz pinched the paper tightly and tossed it into the waste bin. "It'll fade in an hour."

Until then, James appeared half Smurf as the blue brightened to a near glow. He sighed and moved the bottle carefully to the sink.

Eyes hard and pulse quickening, I stared at the garbage can so that Miss Fitz might not notice how angry I'd become. Chet would be graduating in a year, but that meant twelve more months of dealing with his pranks. I'd lost my temper with him and swung at him once, that had been a mistake. I wasn't Serena. The only thing I could do was try to outthink him, but I wasn't James either.

Maybe it was time to come up with a prank ourselves. The field trip would happen when it happened, and Miss Fitz didn't make it seem like the dangerous lesson would be soon. We could come up with a devious plan for Chet.

CHAPTER 3
MISHAP AT THE TREEHOUSE

LATER THAT AFTERNOON, I suggested my plan as we rode our bicycles to Serena's house.

"Sounds good," she said. "Or I could just give him a black eye."

"Miss Fitz wouldn't like that," said James. "It might be best not to antagonize him. He'd know it was us."

Miss Fitz had only one other student; a second-grader, who came alone on Saturday mornings like we all had until after third grade. No one would suspect him of pranks.

"So, we get really clever." I meant James when I said us. "Make it look like an accident."

"Chet will know." James's bike was electric so he glided silently beside me. "It's a bit — *impulsive.*"

Rash, he meant. "That's me," I said, because they all accused me of it. "But Chet deserves it. I don't care if he blames me. Let's just think about it." I knew James was right, but it was fun to imagine getting back at Chet. I wasn't as mad now as I had been.

James shook his head. "You're not considering the consequences. You never do."

Serena pouted but didn't argue the point. She and I usually allied over my more reckless ideas, because they were good. It took us twenty minutes to get to her house and carefully avoid her younger brothers.

"They'll be on their games," she said as we dropped our bikes beside the building her mom used for crafting and slunk into the back yard.

The spring growth had started to bring a deeper green to the woods behind her house, but last year's dead plants still offered plenty of sticky seeds. We'd commandeered an old live oak just in sight of the back porch for our tree house. Her brothers avoided the woods after she'd shown them a tick on her leg. I hated ticks myself.

Our cloaked rope ladder hung between two limbs with the end about six feet off the ground, Serena, the tallest of us, reached it easily. Once she had it in her hand, the cloaking covered her and her backpack even down to her shoes. From where I stood, there was nothing but an old tree with winding branches.

"Clear," she said.

Even three inches shorter than her, I easily found the invisible rung of rope and grabbed hold. In a snap, the cloaking illusion disappeared and the plywood bottom of the tree house appeared. Eight feet long, the ladder hung down the trunk, attached just inside the square hole.

Serena's feet dangled out, then she slid inside. "The caverns," she said.

"What?" I asked. My hair still reeked like a burnt skunk.

James was waiting below me. "She's talking about the field trip. Out by Marianna there's a Bigfoot tribe, but they wouldn't be dangerous."

"Yeah, I guess you're right." Serena sounded disappointed.

We had studied about the Bigfoot tribe, and I would like to meet them. Their magic was better than most humans, supposedly. Not exactly the kind of adventure Indiana Jones would get into. I grabbed hold of the opening cut into the floor of our tree house and pulled up. "Clear."

Our construction had a basic frame of 2x4s, but James had designed it to use the tree branches for support, so the little room swayed with heavy winds. We had IGLOO coolers to keep things dry and to sit on. My old Switch was in one. Serena sat cross-legged in front of her backpack as she rummaged through it. "I brought the wire."

"Romex," James corrected as he climbed.

"Whatever."

I stunk and it was stuffy, so I tossed off my pack and began opening all three windows. The large one led to the side ladder to the roof. All the window covers angled outward to keep out the rain, but this one left enough room to get outside if you moved the netting. "James, you sure about climbing in the tree? Maybe you should have

Serena do it." She was the go to when it came to athletics.

He poked his head inside, lifting his chin as if indignant. "I'll be fine. Better than you."

"True." I wasn't a fan of heights, but neither was James.

"Besides, I was out there last Sunday." His pack squeezed through the opening as he pulled himself inside and spun his legs onto the floor. The entry had a netted hatch that he secured over the top.

We still would have some mosquitoes. It was Florida. By July we'd only come out here at night when we wouldn't roast.

"I remember. That's why I asked." He'd fallen from the perch onto the slanted roof and we'd freaked.

"I'll be fine," he repeated a bit vigorously. He never got angry, but he didn't like us telling him what to do. Well, none of us liked that.

We started laying out the last supplies we'd brought for the project. I had a number of the clamps they used on radiators, though I didn't know what he planned on using those for, and a fresh pack of super long zip ties. James had the last of his red 3D printed wind blades. Serena said they looked like curved axe heads. Along with those he had a round cone-shaped piece with screw holes, which I guessed they attached to.

Serena stood, tapping her lip nervously. "This is a lot to carry up there."

"Tower pole is already in place and the vertical

turbine only weighs about thirty pounds. It won't take up much space." He gave her an excited grin. "Assembly is the easy part."

Now that we were about to have James up in the tree above us again, I questioned how much we needed power in our little room. It had been cool to think of, but what if he fell off? "This is dangerous," I said. "Maybe we tie a rope to you. This can wait until we get rope." I nearly swayed thinking of trying to hold a rope out the window while he plummeted.

"We agreed. And I've thought it all out." James dismissed me as he began stowing parts carefully into a long duffel. Serena exchanged glances with me and grimaced.

I'd been friends with James since before first grade when our moms did playdates. Neither of us had siblings, so we'd spent a lot of time at each other's houses. It wasn't until our parents sent us to Miss Fitz that we met Serena, but the three of us had looked out for each other for six years now. Sending James up into the trees was a bad idea. Even *I* knew that.

He stood and put his hand on my shoulder. "I'm not going to die."

I must have had a really lousy expression on my face, because it took a lot to smile. "I know." Then, to be really assuring, I added, "Please don't."

He chuckled as he slid the duffel over his shoulders like a pack. At the window, he attached a carabiner to a winch cable from his belt to the tool bag that he placed beside the window. With a press of his finger the winch whirred and spit out a few feet of loose wire. "If this gets stuck, help it out."

Serena was pacing wordlessly. She was never quiet unless things were bad.

The screen came off with a rip of Velcro and I shivered at the sound. I watched as my friend climbed out of the window, and he carefully peered up into the tree. Brave was when you did something you knew was dangerous, like Katniss.

I knelt by the edge of the window, watching him climb up the side. Birds called from deeper in the woods and I grimaced at a whiff of my hair in the breeze. After a short bit, the angled flap of plywood blocked my view and I had to rely on his scraping and grunts, along with the rising cable, to know his progress. How high did the turbine need to be?

One heavy limb sprouted from the trunk under the window, probably at level with the bottom of the tree house. Even glancing at that made me queasy with the ground so far below.

"In place," he called down. With a light whir, the cable tightened and his bag of tools 2 pulled up and out of the window. It swung in open air, hit the trunk, and rose.

Serena's pacing behind me covered some of the sound of his work. I sort of wished one of us would talk, but I didn't want to distract him either. My heart began to slow as the minutes passed and my mind drifted back to whatever danger my dad was worried about.

It had to be one of the domains adjacent to

Earth's. The field trip would take us there, surely. Miss Fitz would be with us, she'd said so. How would that bring me second sight? My mom had it. She'd see danger before it happened as a premonition with exact details. Dad had been evasive, but I guessed he either hadn't needed it, or didn't have it.

There was a snap and my heart stopped. With a nasty thud, James fell onto the roof right over my head. Dust puffed out from the wood. Serena and I both winced. "You okay?" I yelled at the ceiling.

The scraping sound as he slid had Serena racing for the window. "James," she yelled.

"Gah!" James cried out in a terrifying blur of color as he fell past the window.

Startled, I thrust out a hand too late. He was far enough away it wouldn't have mattered. Even his tool bag, dangling at the end of the cable, was too far away.

"James," Serena and I both called out breathlessly.

With a grunt, he hit a thick limb below, almost folding over it. I could only stare as he slid down, scrambling to hold onto it. The leaves rustled madly as the thick branch rocked up and down. If he fell off, it was still a long way to the ground.

Suddenly, James stopped with feet dangling and the limb under one arm and his chin. His other hand reached up and grabbed the branch. He couldn't werebear out and hold on during the transmogrification, and even then, the drop might hurt even his tougher form.

"Setun Bar Terrid," I began the lifting spell incantation without a thought. If I could get a grip on him, then it might help him, maybe he could keep from falling.

"No," James said in a tight voice. "My bag. The winch cable."

Finishing the last words of my spell but not activating it, I leaned out, peering down. His tool bag hung six feet under his feet. I could easily lift that to the window. Focusing my will on the bag, I set the spell and began pulling with my fist clenched. It moved quickly, spilling a screwdriver out of the open top.

"Up above you." James said through gritted teeth. "Like a pulley. There's a branch above." He began an incantation of his own, but no one could lift oneself with a spell. He had something in mind.

A lifting spell required sight of the target, and I couldn't see above the window flap. Swallowing, I let the tool bag hang in the air while I reached outside the window to the ladder affixed to the side. My fingers tightened on the rungs and I swung a foot outside, wishing I'd demanded he not go up.

He would have done it anyway. *Stubborn*.

Dangling, I fought a shiver as I pulled my last foot out of the tree house and clung on the side over twenty feet from the ground.

I could see the limb above. When I tried to focus on the tool bag, my eyes zoomed to the leaves and shrubs below, and I couldn't breathe for a full second. James couldn't hang on while I spent time panicking. "Okay," I said mostly to myself. "Over the branch."

Tightening my muscles, I lifted the tool bag through the air and over the limb. James' winch whirred, loosening the cable. That was what he was using his magic on, controlling the winch. He was good at combining his equipment and magic.

Beside me at the window, Serena exhaled in a whoosh, waiting as I relaxed my grip and let the bag glide down to her waiting hands. As soon as she grabbed it, I released my spell fully and shakily restarted the incantation. If I had my staff, my focal, I'd only need a couple words.

"The hammock hook," James said from below.

She scrambled inside, unhooked his bag, and dashed behind me. Metal clinked. "Okay, it's attached." Her voice was steadier than mine had been during the incantation.

I finished my spell and wrapped it around my friend. Cable or not, I was still afraid he'd fall. It took all I had to not look past him to the ground.

The winch whirred and the cable tightened. James used it to get a better grip on the limb and I grunted helping to lift him. In a moment, he had both arms over the wood, then kicked a leg up.

Sweating with the strain of pulling his weight, I watched as he got to his hands and knees, crawling toward me and the trunk. "Move," he said.

He was going to jump for the ladder. I nodded and tried to climb in without releasing the spell, but he weighed too much. "I'll have to let go."

"Do it." He was at the trunk.

I released, and nearly slipped on the rungs. Serena grabbed my arm when I reached for the window. We were still getting my last leg inside when the winch whirred and James hit the side of the tree house.

Pressed against the wall beside the window, I helped her hold James as he climbed back in. Then I flopped to the floor to stare at the ceiling. "I said it was a bad idea."

"Bite me." James dropped beside me.

"What did you do to your face?" Serena asked.

I touched my nose before turning to James. He had a raw rash down his left cheek from just under the eye to his jaw. "Ouch," I said.

"Ouch everywhere. I feel like I might puke."

"It's whatever's in my hair."

He coughed out a laugh. "Likely. You really do stink."

"We need some of Ellie's Salve. I can go get it." Serena reached for her backpack, as if ready to head off for a forty-minute round trip to the classroom. The healing salve was a cure all for scrapes or cuts.

"No, I can go," James said.

"We'll all go." I didn't move though.

"I'll finish the turbine tomorrow. Just had to connect the line."

I leaned up on my elbows. "Not." After nearly losing him, I wasn't going to let him back up in the tree. He'd nearly died. "We don't need electricity."

He winced trying to look at me. "I'm not arguing with you. I don't have the energy. We still have to extend the warding or people will wonder why there's a two-foot-tall red turbine in the tree."

I groaned. It would take us all to adjust the warding. I was tired and reeked. It would be a long trip back to the library before I'd even start home for a well-deserved shower.

CHAPTER 4
THE DEWI SRI

THE JEFFERSON COUNTY LIBRARY was closed by the time we arrived. We made our way to the portal in the back of the building; a section of the wall that only reacted to our presence. The sun sat low in the west and the fresh scent of new growth of late spring wafted in the air.

"Maybe we just wait until tomorrow." James hesitated in the shade.

"Your parents will flip when they see your face," Serena said.

I glanced out at Water Street, but the one car on the road had just passed. "C'mon. She always said to get to her classroom in an emergency." Miss Fitz would be reading. From the rare occasions when she divulged her personal life, we knew she spent it "enhancing her knowledge." When I pressed my hand against the portal, it sucked me through with a flicker of black, and I stepped onto the metal landing of the stairs.

Miss Fitz didn't sit at her desk, where I'd expected her.

Instead, a tall man in an outlandish red-orange hat with a white feather stood at her library shelves across from the desk. He held a silver figurine of a woman with spiky shoulders and a tall crown pouring out a pitcher, though there was no water.

He didn't hear me, and I froze, searching the long classroom for Miss Fitz. *Is this a friend of hers?*

He wore a long jacket the same color as his hat with white lace spilling out of the cuffs and collar. His pitch-black hair curled down over his shoulders. The idol shined as he inspected it.

"Oof," Serena barreled into my back, knocking me to the railing.

The man turned, almost casually. For such a strong chin, he had small, beady eyes. A mustache poked like two thick whiskers out from under his nose to his cheeks. The spiky facial hair pointed higher as a broad smile showed perfect white teeth. "Well, hello." Around his neck hung a glass eyeball on a necklace tucked into the ruffles of his shirt. I didn't trust him.

"Where's Miss Fitz?" I asked.

Serena joined me at the railing. "Put Dewi Sri down. She doesn't like it touched."

He didn't put down the statue but held it firmly as he bowed with a flourish, sticking one white stockinged leg out. "Dr. Emp Donogol, at your service. And you are?"

"Tommy." I grunted as Serena elbowed me.

"Put it down." She shifted away from me with a sniff but didn't head down the stairs.

James spoke from behind us. "Who's that?"

"Dr. Emp Donogol," I whispered.

Serena tucked at my sleeve, then started down the stairs. "Put the goddess back on the shelf. What are you doing in her library?"

I followed, searching the room. Where was Miss Fitz? She made it sound like she never left. Until now, I hadn't considered how odd that might be to live in one room.

When Serena clattered down the steps, Dr. Emp tucked the statue in his jacket pocket as he walked deeper into the classroom. "I really must be away, Dears. So little time to chat with ever so much to do."

"Stop." Serena leaped to the bottom landing.

"No time." The odd man waved a dismissive hand over his shoulder.

"I want you to stop right now." Serena gestured for us to join her, which we were, but this was an adult she wanted to confront. A *tall* adult.

I glanced over my shoulder to James. His scrape was drying up, and he winced as he frowned.

"Want, want, want. Children are always wanting something." Dr. Emp stopped just short of the table where we did our classwork and spun to face us. He breathed out a sigh and spoke slowly with an odd rhythm. "What I would like is for you to join me. Come with me."

I studied him as I kept up with Serena.

His broad smile drooped, he peered about the

room up to the ceiling, and his lips twisted to the side as if frustrated. Had he expected we'd just agree?

"You will put down the statue and leave." Serena came to a stop midway across the carpet, about six paces from him.

"You *really* should join me." He spoke the words in the same slow crooning tone. After a pause, he snorted as if irritated.

I checked the Neverdoor; the door we were never supposed to open. It was closed, but unless Dr. Emp intended to use the head, there was no place for him to go in the back of the classroom. How had he gotten in? Miss Fitz keyed the library portals to respond to us. Did she know him?

"Put it back." Serena crouched almost imperceptibly, but I recognized her "ready" stance from martial arts.

"You can't attack him," I whispered.

"Watch me." She took a step forward. "Back me up."

My eyes widened. The man was nearly twice as tall as I was. Taller than Chet who could set me on my butt with one shove. "Serena?"

"That goddess belongs to Miss Fitz."

"Where is she?" asked James.

Ignoring Serena's crouch, Dr. Emp spun on his heels and began marching for the gray back wall where the Neverdoor sat in the center. He mocked Serena's voice. "Put it back, where is she, I want, and all that nonsense. Insipid children. Can't stand them." He moved quickly and Serena bounded behind him.

"Serena," I called after her, hesitantly springing forward. They thought *I* was rash.

Dr. Emp dashed toward the Neverdoor with his long legs quickly eating up the distance through the alchemy lab, past Miss Fitz's reading chair, and across the open end where we practiced range magic. I stopped chasing when he flung open the door without a care.

I'd never seen inside before. Black mist swirled against shimmering portals of stone and glass. Except for inky fog, there was no floor or ceiling, just a hall of doorways that faded in thickening murk.

Serena skidded to a stop three paces from the door as if she hadn't really expected him to enter. Her hands were balled into fists.

Dr. Emp's boots stirred the mist into eddies as he ran down to a portal on the right. He paused a second to glance back at us. He tapped the brim of his outlandish hat and stepped into the glow to disappear.

James called out when Serena sprang toward the open Neverdoor. "Don't. Where's Miss Fitz?"

"What if he or they took her, before we caught him?" Serena gestured to the classroom. "How did he get in here without her trying to stop him?"

A cold chill rolled up my shoulders and neck. Miss Fitz always told us we were safe here in her classroom. It didn't *feel* safe. "Why do you think they took Miss Fitz? Couldn't she just be shopping or something?"

"She's here in the evenings." Serena turned to search the room.

James tilted his head. "How do you know?"

I studied Serena as she blushed. She had never told us she'd been here outside of class time. I'd mentioned it when I forgot my pack once and had to come back.

"I've come here to study." She flustered and stalked back into the alchemy lab area. "My brothers are too much sometimes." Peering back to Miss Fitz's desk, she headed toward it. "She *should* be here."

"And no one is supposed to be able to get in past the portals." I hadn't even known there were portals on the other side of the Neverdoor. I watched Serena, then turned back to the open door four paces in front of me.

The black mist never escaped past the doorway. It swirled in the corridor, thicker at the edges than the middle, as if to tease us with a glimpse. There had to be a dozen portals visible before the fog was too dense to see any further down the tunnel. If Dr. Emp had done something to Miss Fitz, we had to do something. "We've got to tell our parents."

CHAPTER 5
THE NEVERDOOR

I TURNED BACK to my friends. "Maybe they have a way to contact her." Miss Fitz didn't have a cell phone. We just found her here in the classroom when she scheduled us to be here. "Let's call our parents. They'll know what to do."

James touched his face. "I need the salve."

"Ha." Serena had reached Miss Fitz's desk. "Would she leave voluntarily without her focal wand?"

I glanced at the wall rack where my staff, my focal, hung. Serena's athame and James' tech wand sat on the shelf above. Miss Fitz preferred an old-fashioned wooden wand like my mom and dad. I didn't know if she normally headed outside the class-room with or without it. She'd come by my house plenty of times to talk with my parents, but I didn't think about her otherwise. Honestly, I felt a little crummy that I'd never thought of it.

James nodded to Serena's comment and hurried

to the shelf, picking out the beige jar of Ellie's Salve. I'd used it before; a cool sensation with a mint smell. I still reeked like whatever Chet had put in my hair. Fumbling in my pocket, I pulled out my cell phone and headed toward Miss Fitz's desk.

I called my mom's cell out of habit. "Mom, I'm at Miss Fitz's classroom. She's not here." Drawing in a breath to explain about Dr. Emp, I took too long.

"Why are you there at this time of the evening? Home before dark. She has a life, Tommy." A pan rattled in the background.

"I know. She left her focal." I raised my eyebrows as Serena motioned me to explain quicker or more.

"We don't take our focal everywhere. You know that." Mom's voice had tightened and the background noise stopped. "I'm sure it's fine."

I glared at Serena gesturing in front of me. "There was someone here, Dr. Emp; do you know him?"

Mom took moment before responding. "No. But I don't know all of Miss Fitz's friends."

Serena was pantomiming a goddess statue. I sighed before I spoke. "He took a statue." This wasn't going very well.

"Dewi Sri," Serena blurted out.

"The Dewi Sri statue." I turned toward the shelves mixed with books, fantastical and normal figurines, a picture of Miss Fitz with a teenaged sized dragon and a woman twice her height kneeling beside them with a glass sword on her back. There was a tiara, skulls, feathers, a short Japanese sword, and other things we weren't supposed to touch. Why had Dr. Emp taken that instead of a gold puppy?

"You can let her know about this man and the statue when you go to class tomorrow."

"Mom, doesn't it seem odd to you?"

"As odd as you being there this time of night."

I cringed, watching James lather his cheek. We wouldn't want to mention him almost dying in Serena's backyard. No matter what I said, Mom wasn't running to find Miss Fitz. "Can you call her or anything?"

"She contacts us when needed. Your dad is making dinner and I've got to go help. Home before dark and be careful. Bye, Tommy." A plate rung on a counter, and she hung up.

Serena had her phone out as I turned around. Her lips tight, she focused on dialing rather than me. I couldn't tell if she was upset with me, or the situation. James had the jar back on the shelf and was washing his hands in the sink. I ambled toward him, unsure what I should be doing.

I was at the alchemy lab by the time Serena spoke. "Mother. We need to find Miss Fitz. A strange man stole the Dewi Sri statue off the shelves in her classroom."

James had his phone out but watched Serena.

"She left her focal. He wasn't a friend." Pacing, Serena pointed at Miss Fitz's desk.

What were we supposed to do? After talking to my mom, I was more worried about Miss Fitz than I had been. Curious, I strolled toward the potbelly stove between the alchemy lab and the Neverdoor open to the murky hall.

"What if she needs our help?" Serena scowled at some response. "Okay."

Our parents weren't going to help.

I put my hand close to the teapot on top of the potbelly stove; it was cold. Miss Fitz had an easy chair there. I'd never seen her sit in it. On the other wall was our rack with focals. Chet's was a baseball bat beside my staff.

Empty space stretched out the last fifteen feet before the end of the classroom and the Neverdoor. Scorch marks and soot marred the stone wall from magical range practice.

James cleared his throat. "Mom. Do you know how to get a hold of Miss Fitz?"

I turned back toward the alchemy lab where he stood. Serena stalked toward us with fire in her eyes. We had no reason to believe this Dr. Emp had done something to Miss Fitz, but we didn't have a better explanation either. Going home and forgetting about it didn't seem right.

"Oh, I just wanted to talk to her about a project." Closing his eyes, James swallowed. "No, she's not at the classroom." He shook his head to me and Serena, then his eyes popped open. "No, everything's all right." His eyebrows furrowed. "No, I'm with Serena and Tommy. There's —"

His parents were the most controlling of the three of us. His dad wasn't a witch and knew nothing about magic, so his mom always overreacted hiding it from her husband. Luckily, he was a regional sales manager of something and traveled a lot. Like me, James didn't have any brothers or sisters.

James turned his head down. "Yeah, there was someone in her classroom taking a statue, but he left. We —"

Serena and I watched, waiting for the inevitable. We never should have had James call his parents. He'd have to go home now.

"No —"

I turned and focused on the Neverdoor and the corridor of portals. Could I just leave and not try to find out what happened to Miss Fitz? Knowing how the call would end, I walked toward the opening, not that I'd go in. The swirling black haze left hints of engraved arches around the shimmering glass-like portals.

"Yes." James sounded defeated.

Stopping a pace away, an eddy let a black polished floor appear for a second, then a similar surface on the walls beside the rougher carved border.

"Yes. Yes. Straight home." James hung up and sighed. "I've got to go home now."

CHAPTER 6
THE NEVERDOOR AND NINGA

A GLIMMER of bronze flashed through the mist on the floor of the hall beyond the Neverdoor. I stepped closer, toes at the threshold but not over, and squatted to blow into the thick, black fog where I'd seen a glimmer.

"Tommy?" Serena spoke behind me with an excited pitch. "What are you doing?"

Miss Fitz's bracelet lay two paces inside the hallway. She had come this way and lost it. I imagined Dr. Emp, as large as he was, easily wrestling her into the portal. Her magic was strong though. His might be stronger.

"Is that her bracelet?" Serena asked.

"What?" called out James.

The strange fog rolled up against the threshold, but never entered, as if stopped by a barrier. I reached forward cautiously and touched it. Nothing stopped me. There was no shield or magical force I could feel.

"Tommy, what is wrong with you? Do you know what your problem is? You don't think first." Serena tugged at my shoulder as she chided.

"We have to follow her," I said.

Dr. Emp's words echoed in my head. *What I would like is for you to join me.* I shivered, but stood and stepped over the threshold.

Nothing happened. Serena yanked at my shoulder, but I took a second step. The air was cool and musty smelling.

"Wait," James said from behind.

"I'm just getting her bracelet." I wasn't stepping into that portal — yet. It wasn't rash to be worried about Miss Fitz. The charms were cold and the bell tinkled as I picked it up and backed into the classroom. It was no coincidence that something she never took off had been dropped here.

"What do you think happened?" asked James.

"I can imagine all kinds of things, but it doesn't matter. We have to go after her." I knew they'd argue against another one of my harebrained ideas, but we couldn't leave her with Dr. Emp. I couldn't and knew they wouldn't either.

Serena's lips were tight as she glared at me. They loosened when she finally nodded slowly. "We have to go, but prepared." She gestured toward my staff and our focals on the rack and scanned the room. "Really prepared."

A smile flashed on my face at how quickly she'd supported my idea without argument, then faded at considering whatever fate may have landed on Miss

Fitz. My mind stalled beyond my staff and filling my water bottle. "My goggles!" I beamed and ran to the study area where we kept our notebooks. This was my chance to adventure like Indiana Jones or Amelia Earhart.

Blushing in my excitement, I pulled the old Luxor aviator goggles from 1942 off the shelf. Long ago, I'd replaced the Luxor 12 straps; they stretched down the back of my head as I placed them on my hairline. They were likely useless in this situation, but I'd feel better with them on.

Serena appeared distraught. "I don't have a sword. I should have a sword."

"Well," I studied the room. "What else can we bring?" I asked because she was the one who'd mentioned supplies.

"Healing salves, flashlights." Her list trailed off.

James peered at the bracelet. "I'll need my gear. Drones. Tablet."

"You're going to disobey your parents?" Serena asked.

I knew he'd figure out a way to come with us. We needed his brains, gadgets, and knowledge of magic, matched with her martial arts. What did I add?

He shook his head with an impish smile. "I've got to go home anyway to get equipment. I'll set my gaming monitor to a bot. It'll make just enough noise that my dad will knock at my door and tell me to turn it down. I can set a script to respond with my voice, and a lower volume. I've done it before."

Serena snorted. "You're climbing out your window? Isn't that rebellious?"

His smile faded and he spoke in serious tone. "For Miss Fitz."

———

An hour later, James returned with a tool belt of gadgets, a fat tan backpack, a green pocketed vest, and a box of Nilla Wafers that I grabbed a handful of before we faced the open Neverdoor. In my right hand I held the staff my grandfather had helped me build when I was six. The almost white Hazel tree wood had creamy streaks throughout and a string of runes carved near the top, which named our family witches through his generation, and a thumbnail-sized garnet affixed at the top. In my left hand were a dozen cookies. I'd already broken Rule No.1 in Miss Fitz's classroom.

"Never go in that door." James whispered Rule No. 1. He slid his battery-powered, collapsible focal wand into a special slot in the front of his belt where he could grab it quickly.

After debating with herself, Serena took the short Japanese sword from the bookshelf and carried it in her right hand. She wore her silver and onyx Athame focal tucked in her belt. Her pack hung loose with carefully wrapped potions and salves as mine did.

"Well," I said, then stuffed another wafer in my mouth.

"We might be wrong about which portal she went in," James said.

Serena smiled. "We know where she is." She led the way into the hall, blowing the trails of mist away from her.

"Try not to breathe that stuff." James followed behind me.

A high-pitched, child-like girl spoke from deeper in the hall. "It's not toxic."

Serena drew back her blade, barely longer than her forearm. "Who's there?"

A gray rabbit walked on her hind legs out of the gloom, heading for the second portal where Dr. Emp had gone, and presumably Miss Fitz. "Name's Ninga." Her expression was very humanoid as she frowned and pointed a finger at the shimmer. "That's dangerous. Don't go in there." Around her stomach was a belt of metal links, and from it hung a pouch made of the same loops, just woven in rows. She took another step, as if to go through the portal where she warned us not to go.

"What are you?" asked James.

Ninga smiled and blinked a couple times. "An Oon. That's where we live. Mostly."

I recovered from my initial shock and peered into the depths of the murky corridor as far as I could. "Have you seen an older lady with white curly hair and glasses?"

"Miss Fitz? No."

Serena's mouth dropped open. "You know her?"

"Of course. Very nice lady." Ninga stepped into the tall, engraved portal. Her rabbit form melted into the surface and disappeared, leaving us staring at the shimmering glass.

CHAPTER 7
THE GRAY DOMAIN

I LEAPED to touch the silver surface of the oval portal. Just like the Geology door in the library, my fingers sunk into it, then I was sucked through to the other side. The blackness lasted a moment longer, speeding my pulse. Then I popped out the other side as if ejected.

The air smelled like a gas station with pungent petroleum causing me to expect slicks of oil on the ground. Gray dust stirred under my sneakers. Even the dull sky was a dusty shade of light blue. There were trees ahead, but they had no real color. I could tell leaves from branches by familiar shapes rather than greens or browns.

"Where are we?" James stood at the edge of the portal.

On this side, a shimmering pool circle, more liquid than glass, lay inside a rock frame similarly inscribed with strange markings. It was wider here than in the hall behind the Neverdoor. How did that work?

The rabbit, or Oon, Ninga stood in front of me sniffing the air. "We've got company."

Serena bowled into my back. "Dammit, Tommy."

I stumbled forward, confused about the Oon's statement. Other than some distant mountains and the woods dotting the horizon around us, this seemed like a wasteland of dust.

"Prepare yourselves," Ninga said, taking a step to the side.

The only action either of us took was for Serena to point the short sword at Ninga. "What were you doing out in the hall? Do you know Dr. Emp?"

Ninga spit into the dust. "Vile man. That is one of his Vodynash."

Finally, I followed her gaze to the trees ahead, studying the detail where the lack of color helped to mask shapes.

James grunted behind me. "Where are we?" he asked again.

"The Gray Domain," Ninga replied. She took another step back, nearly at my feet. For rabbits, the Oon were tall, over three feet high.

Squinting, I finally noticed a figure sitting at the edge of the forest, but only because it had begun to move. We were maybe sixty feet away, close enough to make me straighten.

It looked like a man with too big of a smile, small eyes, and not enough forehead. What I thought was gray hair at first, appeared to be a dull fleshy point at the top of its head. As the creature stood, its actual hair hung long from the neck and otherwise shaggy fur covered its body. The feet appeared to have the right number of toes, as did the hands, but they were wider than a human's. From his side, he picked up what appeared to be a mushroom with a long, rigid stem.

What was a Vodynash? *"His Vodynash" – did Ninga mean Dr. Emp's?*

"I'd suggest running," Ninga said. I agreed wholeheartedly, despite my feet seeming to be frozen in place.

"From what?" asked Serena.

I pointed as the creature swung the mushroom head into his fist and we could hear the resounding thud like a hammer into a skull, or at least I imagined that. "The Vodynash."

CHAPTER 8

ESCAPE FROM THE VODYNASH

MY HEART SLAMMED into my throat, making it impossible to breathe. Dr. Emp's Vodynash didn't run, but after two paces its long strides began to eat up the distance between us. Ninga beat a path with her short legs first, then Serena stepped back hesitantly. These creatures must be guards of some type. Why would they work for Dr. Emp?

"Tommy." James's firm voice helped to stir my legs into shaking before I turned. He dashed straight for the portal. At least *he* could move.

And — James bounced off the shimmering surface. He caused ripples though.

I shuffled slowly, as if my panic thawed. The strange world thudded in a hasty beat — no — that was my ears.

Ninga ran delicately past the portal, not at all appearing surprised about any of this. She would have the best understanding of this world.

Serena sprung, sword and Athame ready, after

she saw James's plight. The Vodynash stood twice her height and carried a really nasty sounding mushroom.

Her rash actions seemed to wake me fully. "Run." I gestured to Ninga. "Follow her."

James took the hint quickly, dashing around the portal. We'd have to find a way through eventually. If we found Miss Fitz, she could help us. Our little rescue had crumbled to tatters quickly.

I tugged at Serena's arm and she growled, but eased her stance and turned to come with me. As long as we moved away from the Vodynash, I didn't care where Ninga headed.

Ninga headed for a line of trees. I could make out no other place to hide in the gray dust and rock around with another forest a distance away. Unlike normal woods, the branches hung really low and twisted from one tree into the next. They sprouted fat, round, pale, dusty-green leaves .

Ninga, five paces ahead of me, dove into the branches and they barely seemed to give way. I lost sight of her squirming furry back by the time James followed her in. He pried stiff limbs aside, but clambered over and into the thicket.

"They're hard," he called over his shoulder.

I could hear the Vodynash now, stomping behind me, and picked a different part of the tangle of leaves and branches to sprint to; just a couple feet from where Serena aimed. We would have an advantage over a creature of his size, but not as much as an Oon would. Did Ninga live here?

Stiff didn't begin to describe the branches. I had to push around the ends of them, step over, or climb under to get any distance. In seconds, snapping of wood crashed behind me; I turned to find the Vodynash smashing its metal mushroom into the trees.

"Hurry," I called to Serena, hampered by two weapons. She didn't cut at the woods. That would just have made a path for the creature.

"Planning on it." Her tight voice sounded annoyed.

When I'd mentioned Dr. Emp, Ninga had said "his Vodynash." Whoever the creature belonged to, it didn't stop. Luckily for me and Serena, the limbs barely broke apart as leaves scattered under the smashing of the mushroom club.

With Ninga and James no longer within sight, I could at least hear my friend thrashing ahead. The Vodynash worked at the woods three paces behind me. Serena moved quicker than me, and I only had the focal staff to drag with me. I could mentally stun an opponent with my focal, but it took time to prepare and I wasn't very good with it. My push spell worked well, but I'd never tried against anything that large. It would be better if I kept running — rather, climbing.

"I can see James, not the Oon lady." Dark auburn hair and brown backpack flashed ahead through the bramble.

"Ninga."

"I know."

I hadn't remembered a sun, but the sky's haze

grew shadowed under the thick canopy of leaves rising ten feet above us. The stiff branches threatened to scrape the goggles off my head a couple times, so I pulled them down to hang about my neck.

"Ninga's right ahead of me," James said from just a few yards ahead of us, though I couldn't see him.

I didn't hear the Vodynash anymore. "I think it gave up." My long sigh hinted at how nervous I'd been. Caution was good, so they told me.

"Oh," James said.

"What?" I had visions of the Vodynash surprising us on the opposite side of the thicket of trees. It hadn't been that small.

"A path." His tone was pleased. "Hi."

My heart skipped, wondering who he talked to that I couldn't see through the tangle of limbs and leaves, until Ninga replied. "We can follow this over to the Claymores. We should still keep up a good pace. The Vodynash might give up, or pursue, depending on its commands."

Serena disappeared a second before I lurched out onto a path of packed gray stone cutting through the wall of trees. Branches and leaves formed a ceiling above, but easily left room for me to stand straight.

"C'mon." Ninga took off at a light jog.

James gave us both a quick study, then followed. "I should have sent up a drone when I had a chance."

Serena sheathed her weapons at her sides and darted off to follow. "Shouldn't we be looking for Dr. Emp? Miss Fitz?"

After seeing the Vodynash and the locked portal, I

wasn't sure what we should be doing exactly. "Maybe these Claymores will know." I often ended up in situations where I wasn't sure what to do next, after I'd jumped in. "Ninga, does Miss Fitz come here? Do you know where she might be?"

The Oon ran with short quick steps about two yards ahead of me with James close on her heels. "She visits the settlements on occasion. It's been a fair while since her last time here."

"She goes to the Claymores?" asked James.

"Oh, yes. It's closest to the portal."

"That you can enter?" He gestured with his hand, though she couldn't see him.

"Very easily." Ninga flashed a smile over her shoulder. A rabbit smiling proved odd — and disturbing.

"How? I couldn't get through. Is it keyed to you?"

"Yes, keyed to me. I've always been able to go through."

Maybe she could open it for us. Not that we'd leave until we searched for Miss Fitz. I tried to align my sudden experience to one of my heroes, perhaps Indiana Jones. It sounded so much more fun in books.

A dull gong echoed far in the distance. I barely heard it over our feet scuffing the gravel.

"Oh, my." Ninga sped to nearly a run.

"What is it?" I asked. I didn't want it to be what I guessed.

"Dr. Emp's alarm. I'm guessing he found out you were in his domain."

CHAPTER 9
WINDING TRAIL TO THE CLAYMORES

I SUCKED in deep breaths after the climb through the tight forest and the jog down the winding path. My chest tightened with each ringing of the distant gong. "Does that mean more Vodynash will be searching for us?"

"It very much does," Ninga said. Her little arms pumped at her side now. "The Claymores will only be safe for a while. He'll expect us to go there."

I didn't ask how far away we were, nor where we'd go to hide afterward. A short break would be all I could ask at this point. We'd quickly gone from hunting to hunted.

"We need to find Dr. Emp," Serena said. "Do you know where he is?"

"They say his fortress is past the stone flats. Oon aren't treated well there." She shivered as she said the last part.

"Where are the stone flats?" Serena's voice had a sharp edge to it. I'd never seen her this agitated, but she'd never had a real opportunity to use her martial skills before, and we were running away.

Ninga gestured to our right and back. Serena's sharp glance at the wall of trees there made me wonder if she truly intended to just march up to Dr. Emp. I didn't feel confident about doing that after seeing the Vodynash, but we had to do something.

"We need to be careful," I said.

Serena scoffed. "Coming from you."

"He's right," huffed James.

Tired and winded as him, I nodded silently.

Serena didn't seem to be having any trouble running, but she spent a lot of time at the martial arts studio while James and I played games. Her mom took her and her brothers to Tallahassee two or three nights a week for their classes. Part of me felt jealous that she had brothers and spent so much time with her mother, but she'd also lost her dad to a car accident before she really knew him. James and I still had our dads, but his traveled for work. I couldn't complain.

"I've got drones." James spoke in short bursts between breaths. "If we get somewhere clear I can get us a view. We can find the safest routes."

"I like that," I said. Not running into another Vodynash would be preferable. We had come here with no real understanding of where we were going, or what we were up against. "Who is Dr. Emp?"

"He is the ruler of the Gray Domain." Ninga's tone was polite, but dismissive.

"Always, or did he come here?" If we had to fight his minions, we should know what to expect.

She sighed ahead of me, then replied in quick sentences. "He was not always here. It is believed he came from your domain. He is a wizard, of sorts. You should ask others what his powers truly are. I know he gained control of the Vodynash, and they thrive under his command. The Oon do not fare as well. Many Oon serve him at his castle." Her tone was bitter at the last statement.

"Willingly?" I asked.

"Not at all. His Vodynash raid settlements and take Oon away."

"That's horrible." I bristled and for a moment hoped Serena got a chance to stab him.

"They are taken not just to serve." Her voice was quiet.

James gasped. "To eat?"

"Yes."

I flushed at the thought, then remembered I'd considered her no more than an odd rabbit at first, until she spoke. There'd been no birds in the sky, little grass to speak of, so perhaps there weren't cows or many other animals. It would seem a rude question to ask in this conversation. I caught a slight whiff of Chet's stink potion, but it had faded and I'd forgotten about it once we'd arrived through the portal.

"Maybe Miss Fitz came here to stop him," Serena said. "Someone has to."

I did want to see the end of such a horror, but

what could we do against a wizard? "Has anyone ever tried to stop him?" I asked Ninga.

"I don't believe so, but the domain is large. Is that what you came to do?" Ninga asked.

"No," I admitted. An extra layer of guilt made me blush. "We're here for Miss Fitz."

"And the Dewi Sri," Serena added with ferocity.

Morose, we continued to run until sunlight lit a bright patch of the trail ahead where the trees thinned on the right. Thin grass grew at the edges where the gravel ended. Each stride made the opening clearer. I wouldn't be able to run much longer and the ringing gong had stopped echoing around us. We needed a rest to plan.

I hoped it was our destination, but then Ninga slowed to a stop, raising a paw so we slowed as well. Our feet scuffed through gravel, then fell silent. Only our breaths sounded in this quiet world of strange trees and nightmarish creatures, and mine was ragged from our hasty escape.

Muffled through the trees, something growled and gnashed. Ninga had very good ears if she'd heard it over our running. The high-pitched scream that followed rose over any other noise.

She snapped her attention to us, studying with a sudden intensity. "Can you fight?" she asked. Her ears tilted back and her face had an unexpected fierceness.

Serena drew blades with a rasping scrape; I grimaced and raised my focal staff. James pulled out his collapsible wand, flicking it so that the metal sections extended out to a foot-long wand with the end shining. We'd prepared for trouble, but then run from the Vodynash.

Ninga nodded and sped down the trail, hopefully not toward a Vodynash. "It sounds like a Taar. They're brutes, but dumb."

Not a Vodynash. The sounds grew louder and high-pitched voices called out above the more guttural sounds of a beast. We arrived at the opening in our trail with weapons ready, then paused gaping at the sight before us.

The clearing was wide with more than a dozen mud homes rising from the dust and rock. Paths led off into the same dense trees surrounding the low, round dwellings. Frantic Oon scampered around the houses, some were already bounding into openings in the forest on the far side. A small group stood their ground heroically with spears, and one crawled bleeding toward a clay mound.

However, ten yards ahead of us writhed an impossible fifteen-foot long worm with reddish scales and a four-foot high circular mouth. Rows of teeth gnashed as the Taar lunged after the few fighting Oon and their tiny sticks. They did little more than distract it and jump out of the way. Some threw rocks from a safer distance.

Stubby for a worm, its tail pushed it about, but there were no eyes, only a ring of whiskers about the gaping and snapping maw. The orifice stretched impossibly from a puckered close to a wide teeth flashing gape. I swore there was a sharp smell like a marsh in the air.

Pointed sticks just scratched at the Taar's dusty scales. I wasn't sure a bullet would stop it, if we had one. A bazooka or hand grenade would be my weapon of choice. My staff's fireball might give it pause, if I could get it to aim right. I was very weak on explode or slash, but it was worth a try.

Serena yelled and ran forward with her sword raised and her Athame pointed toward the Taar.

CHAPTER 10
THE TAAR

"SERENA," I called out. We were witches, we didn't need to dive in with sharp things and karate kicks.

The Oon fighting the Taar noticed us for the first time, backing away. This left the creature turning and somehow noticing her, though without eyes, I couldn't imagine how. It might have been her screaming at it.

I scuffled to the side to get a better, angle; one without Serena in line, and prepared a spell I was proficient in; slowing. It didn't stop anyone like stun might, but I was lousy at stun.

Focusing like Miss Fitz had trained me, I willed the staff with my magic. It never felt like anything happened, but if I didn't give it the attempt it wouldn't work as well. "Sebis Halaal," I said as I tilted my staff at the beast. Miss Fitz said it didn't help to point, except to make the user center their magic better.

I could always feel the magic, but it felt strongest when I did well. It rushed through my body like ripples of watery electricity. There were no cool lights or sonic booms, but I knew my spell hit the Taar.

It did nothing. Okay, I was average at the slow spell. Worse was fire or explode. They rarely hit what I intended. Push was my best, I'd try that next.

The beast snapped at Serena just as fast as it had with the Oon. She expected it though and leaped to the side, slashing at its now closed lips, or whatever they were. Her blade marked a black line about two inches on the mouth, dropped a whisker, and slid uselessly against the scales. The Taar roared and the Oon were obviously impressed.

James called out, "Rashk Nevid." His stun was the best of the three of us. Like my spell, there was nothing to see, but his seemed to have some minor effect as Serena darted in with a cut into the Taar's open mouth before it clamped down.

The Oon had moved back nearly to their homes, but they kept watching Serena. One helped the wounded one inside, though I doubted dried mud would stop the Taar.

With another strike, Serena caused a thin black line at the top of the creature's lip, but despite a momentary reaction to James's spell, it hadn't really slowed much. When it roared again, Serena threw a fireball from her Athame straight into its throat. The red-orange ball of fire was about the size of her head and it flew with a satisfying crackle from the tip of her Athame.

This, at least, got a decent reaction from the Taar. Wisps of fire splashed along rows of teeth with a whoosh and even steam. The creature rolled and gnashed twice wiggling back toward her. It did not seem hurt in any real fashion. A little black scorched some of the already gray teeth.

"Xaban Sait." I sent the push spell through my focal as Serena lunged in to slice at the Taar's lip again. My magic had some slight impact, but considering its size and likely weight, the force of using it toppled me back onto my butt. Push and lift reacted against a witch's own body in corresponding measure, less so with a focal. Miss Fitz and James called it "reciprocating," but Serena and I called it payback.

While I scrambled back to my feet, James tried his stun spell with better results than mine. Some might expect him to transmogrify into a bear, but he was a cub. He'd never shifted in front of us except for the one time I talked him into it when we were ten. I certainly didn't expect him to do it now.

Serena got in three more slashes with the sword. A number of whiskers were scattered in the dust now, like fat worms with no mud.

A stun spell needed to hit nerves, and from our positions, James and I were hitting the side of its mouth. Slow worked on all cells, best on muscle. Stun on brain cells. Miss Fitz had explained it in more technical terms.

I turned to Ninga who stood at the opening of the trail. "Where is its brain?" I asked.

"Back of its throat." She opened her mouth and pointed.

I scurried over to James as Serena danced with the Taar. "We're aiming stun at the wrong place. It's at the back of its throat."

He nodded thoughtfully. "Like an earthworm."

"Sure. Earthworm." I glanced at the chubby, scaled Taar, not seeing the resemblance. "So we get close and when it opens its mouth, we try and stun it back there."

James raised his eyebrows. "That sounds — dangerous."

"We can't let it eat Serena, or the Oon."

"Dangerous — and rash." He squinted at Serena. She and the Taar had danced until they were sideways to us. "We might have to do it though." He pulled out a nine-inch tube from his belt. "Then we could use this." He pushed a button and a three-pronged grappling hook popped out.

"To do what?"

"Snag the brain and maybe damage it."

The entire contraption was maybe a foot and a half long. "Are we supposed to climb inside the mouth and stab it?"

He chuckled. "Air-compressed. It'll shoot the full length of a ten-yard cable that holds almost two hundred pounds. It's for climbing."

Serena squealed and we both jumped. She rolled across the ground just out of reach of the Taar and sent another fireball into the side of its cheek.

"Serena, we have a plan," James said.

"Sounds great." She kept focused on the Taar.

"We need to all throw stun spells to the back of its throat." He sounded confident, but neither Serena nor I were very good at that spell.

"Okay." Her drawn-out response hinted at her doubts.

"That's where its brain is," he explained.

"Of course." She dodged a snapping maw. "Let's try it."

"We need to all be in front of it."

Serena leaped to the side with another strike. "That's going to be difficult. It moves kind of fast."

James backed up two steps. "Run to me. It'll follow."

I readied my staff, eyes wide at the thought of its chomping maw aimed at me. Serena cocked her head as if unsure, then darted back to stand in front of James and I.

As the Taar growled and wiggled forward, it finally opened its mouth wide as if to take us all in at once. I imagined my uncle George at a buffet.

We spoke in unison. "Rashk Nevid." I aimed into the darkest center of the throat, hoping James and Ninga were correct.

It worked. The tail stopped and the mass of the Taar brought the creature to a stop in a low cloud of dust. James's device popped, sending a flash of metal into the depths. It didn't go far into the dark maw as a squishy slap left a slack on the cable coming out of James's tube.

"Grab it and pull," he said.

"What?" I asked, but I was already reaching for the cable with him and Serena.

She smiled. "We're going to yank its brains out."

"Maybe," James corrected. "If we hit it or near it." He checked to see if we all had a grip. "One — two — three."

CHAPTER 11
GOING FORWARD

SOMETHING RIPPED out of the Taar, and we stumbled back nearly falling. As it flew out to land at our feet, I grimaced at the red-black shreds attached to the barbs of the hook. The creature shuddered in what I hoped were death throes.

The three of us stepped back, even Serena though she held her sword ready. The Oon were not as confident and continued to hide, other than Ninga still at the opening of the trail.

James left the hook in the dust, but still held the tube. "I think that did it." He shivered. "We really aren't equipped to handle Taar and Vodynash."

"Miss Fitz would have stopped it with magic." I agreed with him, but I also wondered how she was doing, if she was even here. It didn't really matter since we couldn't get back through the portal. We also had the Vodynash searching for us.

The Oon settlement, the Claymores, was silent except for the last twitches of the Taar. I couldn't find one of them. Even the wounded one had been dragged into a mound. The sky had no sun or clouds, just a dull uniform haze.

I turned to Ninga. "Can you take others with you through the portal?"

Her eyebrows raised. "I don't know. No one has ever wanted to go."

Who would want to stay here?

"We can't leave until we find Miss Fitz and get back her Dewi Sri." Serena was adamant, but less sure of herself than before, at least about our teacher. She didn't glower at me.

James continued to stare at the Taar. "We can't fight these or the Vodynash. We'll starve. Is there water here?"

Ninga gestured to the settlement. "The Claymores have a well. The Oon have built many. The water is not deep."

The comment prompted me to reach for my water bottle tucked in the side pocket of my backpack. We really hadn't prepared enough.

"We shouldn't stay here," James said. He turned to face us and nodded to Ninga. "You said they would come here first to search."

"They'll likely be guarding the portal." I glanced at Ninga for confirmation. She nodded once.

Serena spoke with an air of confidence that I didn't feel. "Then we are careful and sneak to the castle to search for Miss Fitz. If we can find her, then her magic will help us get out — after we get the Dewi Sri."

James looked to me, as if I was to decide. I didn't see a lot of options, but I didn't know if Serena's plan was the best. Spending the rest of my life in the gray domain wasn't my idea of a choice at all. "Let's put a drone up in the air. Ninga, how long do you think we have before the Vodynash will be here?" I asked.

She peered at the woods. "They can run fast, but they might not organize very quickly. Until Dr. Emp, they rarely hunted these woods. I would not rest long."

As James pulled off his backpack, I drank water and studied the mud domes. A few Oon peeked out through the entrances to watch us. Considering our attack on the Taar, they might be grateful, but also wary of Serena's sword and our magic. With the beast dead, I expected some of them to come out. Ninga was obviously with us.

Producing a tiny drone from a small case, James set it in the dust and pulled out his tablet. "It will only last seventeen minutes."

"Which direction are the stone flats?" I asked Ninga.

She gestured across the clearing to the opposite side. There was an opening in the trees there, and I assumed a trail. James studied his tablet, then the drone whirred, hopping up to head height before rising slower. He held the screen lengthwise at his waist guiding it with his thumbs on controls at the side. A quick image of us disappeared and he spun it at the treetops. The area behind us was a dusty expanse with gray-green forests dotting the edges.

In the direction of Dr. Emp's were more forests with occasional clearings. As our view rose, grayer open areas spread out into a hazy horizon of distant mountains. We raced over the woods spotting another Oon settlement with them milling about mud domes. A couple of the inhabitants peered up at us.

"Are the Taar common?" I asked Ninga. The tree canopy was too dense for me to see inside.

"Not at all." She appeared engrossed in the view. The Oon would never have seen technology like this most likely.

At the right edge of the screen, dust trailed up on a stretch of open area with gentle slopes. The drone tilted and flew in that direction. Two Vodynash, carrying their mushroom-head clubs, loped across the terrain. Glancing in the sky, I could not see the drone anymore, but pointed to my right. "Are they over there?" The trail we had taken might lead in that direction.

James barely shifted to see where my arm pointed. "Yes. Not really very far away either."

I drew in a tight breath. "Okay. See if you can see these stone flats."

The view veered to the left, but forest just trailed through large open areas. Another Oon settlement was obvious with its mud domes. The horizon was still a haze that could have been stone flats, or more dust and trees. Another pair of Vodynash running from that direction left a plume of dust rising into the gray sky.

"We won't know if they're on the trails." It was an obvious statement, but our biggest danger. "Ninga, can you lead us to the next settlement on the way to the stone flats?"

Oon didn't have much in the way of shoulders, but she shrugged. "I can do that."

Serena nodded in agreement with me as James spun the drone about and headed back toward us without argument. Knowing him, he had a case of batteries and a backup drone if not two. If needed, he could have gone down one of the winding trails.

I continued to watch, getting a sense of the terrain ahead and finally a view of the expanse again behind us. The dim shape of the portal waited there; useless to us. We really had to find Miss Fitz to get out of here. I didn't like the sound of Dr. Emp's "fortress," as Ninga had called it.

"We're going to have to be very careful," I said, more to myself than anyone else. "We need to go forward."

"Agreed." Serena smiled and finally sheathed her sword and Athame, reaching for her water bottle.

James sighed and took a pause. "Agreed." He chuckled. "You almost sound cautious. Are you okay?"

I laughed somewhat bitterly, staring at the dead Taar. "Not at all."

CHAPTER 12
THE HUNT FOR MISS FITZ

I WATCHED as an Oon finally exited a mud dome toward the back of the settlement, marching toward us. They were mottled gray with more white than Ninga's fur. "Who's that?" James's drone descended as it sped over the trees toward the settlement. The Oon glanced up with a start at the noise.

"Gachin. She's the Mother of the Claymores."

I blinked. "Like mother of all these Oon?"

Ninga laughed. "No, it is her position as elder. She speaks for them."

The drone reached us before Gachin did, considering the wide berth she gave the dead Taar. The device dropped into James's hand and he knelt to extract the battery.

Gachin stood taller than Ninga by an inch or two. Her black eyes flicked from me to James and Serena before settling on Ninga. She came to a stop three yards away. "Traveler Ninga. You bring visitors."

"They are from the portal. The Vodynash hunt them."

The Mother glanced at the trail opening behind us. "We heard the alarm. Is it wise to bring them here?" She shook her head, shifting focus back to the Taar. "I am sorry. We appreciate your timely arrival."

"Have you seen Miss Fitz?" Serena asked.

The Oon clasped her hands over her stomach and tilted in what might have been a slight bow. "I am Gachin, Mother of the Claymores, Wind of the Houses, and Leg of Leaves."

Serena raised her water bottle in salute. "Serena. Miss Fitz?"

"I have not seen her for two seasons of Storms, Serena." Gachin turned to me expectantly. Her hands remained at her stomach and she showed no signs of getting closer to us. We probably reminded her of Vodynash or Dr. Emp, though she spoke of Miss Fitz with the same positive tone that Ninga used.

"Uh, Tommy of Monticello, ma'am." I wasn't about to make up titles, but it sounded right. My bow was a bit exaggerated.

James snapped the case of his drone shut. "James. Pleased to meet you." He was hurriedly packing up, but hadn't touched the hook draped with Taar flesh.

Gachin addressed Serena. "Miss Fitz is here? Why did she not visit? Do the Vodynash search for her?" Her eyes flicked to Ninga.

Serena capped her water. "We think so. Dr. Emp stole something from her and we can't find her."

"Beyond the portal?"

"Yes we followed him in — after we believed Miss Fitz went in the portal too." Serena added the last part as an afterthought and didn't mention the bracelet. "We met Ninga in the hall."

"So, you are not sure she is here at all?" Gachin frowned, whiskers rising. "Why would you follow Dr. Emp? He is a dangerous and evil man."

"You have never met him, Gachin," Ninga said. "Luckily. You are right though. They are determined to follow him, and if Miss Fitz is actually here and needs help, I am happy to aid them. The Vodynash will search here first, as close as you are to the portal."

"Don't worry, we aren't going to stay here." I hated that we were bringing the Vodynash down on the Claymores. I also wondered about our plan to get any closer to Dr. Emp than we needed to. "Maybe just get some water from your well."

Gachin checked the Taar again. "Yes. Of course." They might be stuck with its rotting corpse, but first they had to evade the Vodynash.

James shrugged into his pack, pulling his water bottle out. "Thank you." He started chugging and didn't seem nearly as winded now from our race down the trail.

The Mother gestured to the center of camp and strode off ahead of us. "Ready. Ready. The Vodynash will be here. They are looking for these three, but we will not risk any of ours."

I flushed at her comment and hoped we didn't

bring disaster to everyone we met. From Ninga's explanations, they already had a hard life.

Cringing, James wiped the hook off against the gray dust, tapping off chunks. I didn't envy him and might have left it behind.

Serena kept drinking as she followed Ninga toward the center, and I turned to trail behind them.

Oons of all sizes and various colors peeked out of doorways and trees around the clearing. In a moment, those in the woods trotted toward domes while all but a couple of the younger and more curious disappeared deeper inside.

Gachin called out strange names and gave those Oon more directions about what to take and what to leave as she led us between two domes. Inside one home was the sound of scurrying. From a doorway, an Oon raced out with a basket. By the time Serena and I reached the well, the settlement was a beehive of activity, though none of the Oon ventured too close to us.

A foot tall wall of mud rising from the edge of a three-foot wide hole. The well had a pole centered across the middle with a rough rope tied to the middle that dropped down to the water below. I had never used a well, and though I doubted Serena had, she knelt beside the wall and grabbed the rope.

James approached with his water bottle while his head flicked about watching the Oon. "Miss Fitz has never mentioned them. I've never found them described in any of her books."

Rabbits who could weave baskets, stab at Taar, or

build wells had never been discussed. "Maybe she didn't want us to know what was behind the Never-door. We might have been crazy enough to come peek." I could easily see myself doing that, unless I'd known about the Vodynash. They scared me.

"Well, we know what she did when she wasn't teaching." Water sloshed deeper in the well as Serena pulled up the rope, hand over hand.

"Makes me wonder if she's even here," James said.

"We found her bracelet in front of the portal. She wouldn't have just dropped it and not noticed." Serena shifted her movements away from the center bar, and the edge of a clay pail was visible. "Get your bottles ready, this thing leaks a bunch of water."

I laid down my staff, and we moved to the short wall of the well with our bottles opened. The more I heard about Dr. Emp and his Vodynash, the less I liked the idea of going to his fortress. "What if we are wrong about her being here?"

Serena spoke in a growl. "I'm not giving up that easily. On Miss Fitz, or the Dewi Sri"

My lips tightened, I hadn't intended to give up *entirely*. "Well, we don't know that she's there – at the fortress."

Her eyes grew cold. "No, we don't know for sure, but Dr. Emp took the Dewi Sri. We know where it will be. While we check to see if Miss Fitz is there, we can at least get that back. It's something important, or she wouldn't have it on those shelves."

I winced. I didn't care about the stupid statue.

Serena wouldn't back down on that topic, I could tell. "How about we just search around here for her, then go to the fortress as a last resort?"

Nostrils flaring, she focused on her task, not answering my question.

The odd-shaped bucket had one side slightly lower than the other. It appeared intentional. The rope was knotted through holes on each side and she easily tilted it to pour clear water into our bottles. "We split up. You and James play it safe checking the Oon settlements, and I'll go get the Dewi Sri – and check to see if Dr. Emp has Miss Fitz."

I glanced at James, not to see if he agreed with her plan — neither of us would let her go alone— but hoping he could persuade her.

He didn't meet my eyes. "It's not like we can go back. I don't think we should split up. Miss Fitz will get us home, if we find her."

I sagged. "Do you believe we'll find her at the fortress?"

"Based on the bracelet and Dr. Emp's presence in her classroom, I think she's here." He turned to Ninga standing beside Gachin. "Where does Miss Fitz usually go when she comes here?"

Ninga frowned, tugging her whiskers forward. "Here, the Claymores are the closest to the portal."

James met my eyes. "Logically, if she is here, and she didn't visit the Claymores, then someone has intercepted her. The only person who could do that is Dr. Emp, or his Vodynash."

He made sense, but I resisted the notion of getting

ourselves into that kind of situation. *What would Indiana Jones do?* "Then we go to the fortress and hunt for Miss Fitz."

We had all three bottles brimming when she lowered the bucket quickly to the bottom. The Oon had thinned out around us, except for Ninga talking with Gachin. Those leaving didn't go in the various openings leading to trails, but climbed directly into the branches and leaves. After our one encounter with a Vodynash, it was probably the safest course.

James pulled out his tablet as we approached the two Oon. He had an image of the edge of the settlement and the woods trailing off toward the horizon. "I think we'll be using that exit," pointing at the opening ahead of us. He then drew a line across his picture to another settlement just visible on the screen.

Gachin pulled back as we approached. "Sure legs, Ninga."

Our guide returned the greeting before the Mother of the Claymores dashed away. She pointed toward the opening James had guessed would be our path. "Are you sure about this?"

I shook my head. "Not at all, but we're going to do it anyway."

Ninga trotted away, and we followed her toward Dr. Emp and his fortress.

CHAPTER 13
STICKS AND STONES

I WAS SOMEWHAT relieved that we didn't have to race when we reached another winding trail inside the trees, until Ninga spoke from the front of our group. "Keep your ears high, we don't want to run into a pair of Vodynash in a rush."

My toes scuffed against the gravel and James tripped, nearly falling down. "You think they'll be coming down this path?" I asked. It did make sense, if we were heading toward Dr. Emp, then they would take this path to the Claymores coming from that direction. "Is there another way?" Perhaps we should have had this conversation before we left the settlement. It wasn't too late to go back.

"We'll hear them," Ninga said.

Now that I wasn't running for my life, and instead running toward danger, I studied the forest. I'd noticed the sparse grass before, but there were other plants among the trees. In the same pale green, there were clumps the size of my fists with tiny leaves like my dad's Chia pet, but without the face of some painter. Thin vines trailed some of the branches, appearing to have no leaves or reaching the ground for roots. The gray domain was a strange place. I didn't want to be stranded here.

"What is the name of the settlement we're heading for?" I considered asking what the Oon ate, but I assumed it was the grass, because — well, rabbits.

"Derrymeres." Ninga probably didn't want to talk, listening to the trail ahead for Vodynash.

I frowned apologetically, but only James noticed. The woods around were quiet with no birds or squirrels causing a racket, maybe not even bugs. No mosquitoes would be nice. Our feet made a lot of noise on the gravel.

We'd run without talking for about ten minutes, and I wished I'd asked how long it would take to get there before we started. It felt awkward to say anything now. Just when I had decided I could risk speaking, Ninga's ears twitched and she skidded to a halt, rather noisily.

Even when we stopped, I didn't hear anything. She, however, dove into the trees at our left. We all followed without a question and made a horrible racket climbing through the branches. Serena had her sword out, of course. After taking down the Taar, I began to wonder if we could face a Vodynash if we had to.

Settling into crunching dead leaves below the branches, I found my first bug. It was too large. The size of my thumb, it had big pincers and a dozen legs. Gray, of course, its body was like a beetle but sprouted whiskers off the shell. Two feet from my face, it chewed on a leaf. We'd climbed right over it.

I stared at it while the crunching footsteps sounded from down the trail. They seemed to be spaced oddly until my brain sorted out two pairs of feet running across the gravel, getting closer with every stride. My chest tightened slightly, but they were moving too fast to be searching the woods around them.

Something tickled my leg. My heart raced as I imagined a fat beetle crawling over my skin, perhaps stopping for a nibble. If the heavy footfalls weren't so close, I would have shaken it off or sat up to whack at it. Instead, I stared wide-eyed in the direction of the trail, holding my breath and waiting for another tickle. It never came.

Two gray Vodynash stormed past us, on their way to the Claymores. I barely saw them, just a glimpse of motion, then their footsteps running away from us. Wanting to dig at my legs and make sure nothing had settled on me, I drew in a deep breath. A sharp scent, like sweat, stung my nose.

It took far too long before Ninga rustled leaves as she rose. I rolled to my side, examining my legs, but there was nothing except a few broken pieces of debris. Shivering, I brushed them off. "Are we safe now?" I asked.

"If no more Vodynash are following them," said Ninga as she picked her way toward the trail.

I rose, keeping an eye on the bug. "That sounds like a no."

"No, then." She said.

We crawled back through the branches and leaves, stepping onto the gravel. "How far to the Derrymeres?"

"A few more minutes." Ninga waited until we all stood on the trail, then jogged in the direction we'd been heading before the Vodynash had arrived.

"We're going to stop there?" asked Serena.

"We'll cross through their settlement." Ninga kept her voice low. "The trail on the other side is more direct than this one. The Vodynash likely came down it."

I had worried about the Claymores, but at least they'd had a warning. "Would the Vodynash have searched the settlement? Hurt the Oons?"

"Hmm. Searched perhaps, but they wouldn't linger." She took a few more strides before she continued. "Hopefully no one was hurt."

Barely five minutes after hiding from the Vodynash, an opening let the strange pale light onto the trail. Ninga was the first to reach the exit and slow to a stop. I followed close behind her and was nearly skewered when a rough-hewn wooden spear flew at my face.

"Hey!" I dodged, stepping into Serena right behind me.

A scowling Oon stood four yards away, disappointed I'd avoided his attack. The three behind him were tossing stones.

Ninga had raised her arms, waving them to stop. "No, no. Visitors."

I took a solid whack to the forearm, but they weren't throwing very hard and the stone had been two-inches big. Serena pulled her sword.

"Stop." I put my arm in front of her. "They just had the Vodynash run through here, let Ninga explain."

Serena glared at me, but nodded.

A couple more Oon were running to join the four defenders, but they held their spears like they were going to use them, rather than toss them in our direction. I was lucky I hadn't lost an eye.

"Dumatid, they are friends of Miss Fitz," Ninga explained. "They are searching for her. The Vodynash are after them."

The Oon who'd tried to kebab me, Dumatid, glowered and didn't appear deterred. I had no doubt he'd try again, if his spear wasn't on the trail behind me. "Then they are the cause of this."

James stepped up beside me. "Have you seen Miss Fitz?" he asked.

His question calmed the Oon more than Ninga's statement had. They glanced to each other, then Dumatid answered. "She is here?"

"She's missing. We think she might have been forced here." James was calmer than I felt.

"Dr. Emp stole from Miss Fitz." Serena still had

her sword out. "We think he took her to his fortress, we're on our way there now."

"Dr. Emp steals from all of us." Dumatid relaxed, but he peered longingly at his spear, so I retrieved it. "He takes bodies and minds."

I paused before tossing the sharpened stick to his feet. "Minds?"

Dumatid snatched up his spear. "Yes, minds. He can speak words, and you will obey. The Oon obey. The Vodynash obey."

I thought about how oddly he spoke. Had he done that with Miss Fitz? We hadn't been affected.

Ninga was nodding. If she'd known, why hadn't she said anything? We might be immune, or maybe his power didn't work outside of the Gray Domain. *She could have warned us.*

Serena put away her sword as more Oon were popping out of the surrounding woods with curious expressions. The clay domes and settlement looked identical to the Claymores, but there were more exits into the surrounding trees.

I didn't see any wounded Oon or any sign of a fight. "Did the Vodynash come through here? We saw them on the path." My pulse had slowed since no one was throwing spears and rocks at me, but my chest remained tight.

"They did. We heard their alarm and prepared before they arrived. If they are searching for you, they may come back." Dumatid glanced at the warriors beside him. "We will keep everyone safe."

When Ninga led us to another opening in the trees, I couldn't shake the anxious feeling. Dr. Emp could talk people into doing what he wanted. We couldn't protect against that. As bad, Ninga hadn't warned us.

CHAPTER 14
THE STONE FLATS

JAMES and I were losing steam as we trekked through the next stretch of forest. We were heading toward an impossible scenario, and our Oon escort kept a quick pace.

"The next chance we get, I'd like to send up my drone again." He didn't speak to any of us in particular, but it seemed like a good way to gauge how much farther we had to go. Ninga didn't have a concept of distance that related beyond the time it took to run there.

We were headed for a settlement of Oon called Biddies. "When we get to the Biddies, you should launch it." It was a weird name, but today was all about weird.

He didn't seem to notice. "I'd like to see this terrain of the stone flats. It sounds simple enough, but not everything here has been as it seems."

We came to a split in the tree-covered trail and Ninga swiftly shifted us to the left where a curve threatened to lead us back the way we came. "Are we still headed toward the stone flats and Dr. Emp?"

Her ears bobbed, perhaps in a nod. "Yes. These woods will continue around beside it to other settlements, but many of those closest to the stone flats are empty." Her paw waved in a general direction ahead and to the right.

"Because of Dr. Emp?" Serena's tone was sharp.

"Yes. His Vodynash hunted there the past few cycles, they move deeper all the time." The path curved slowly back so as if heading toward the flats she'd pointed to.

"Do you think the Vodynash came this way?" James was right to ask since we'd nearly run headlong into them before.

"I doubt it." Ninga dodged us through a set of winding curves that left us little visibility of the trail. "I hope not."

I didn't ask why she hadn't mentioned Dr. Emp's ability to control Oon and Vodynash. She had offered little we didn't ask about. We had to hope there wasn't anything we didn't know to ask.

The opening to the Biddies came up quickly, and when we stepped into their settlement they were caught off guard. Cries broke out, even as we let Ninga step forward while we waited at the woods. Some ran for the surrounding woods, some for clay domes, and a few for spears. I really wished we had learned the shield spells before heading out, as they might stop pointed sticks and rocks. The air smelled musty.

Ninga had made it almost to the first dome when an unarmed Oon approached her with hostile looking warriors racing to take position at her sides. Those with spears glared at us, not Ninga.

James peered up at the sky, no doubt longing to release his drone, but we waited patiently. Even Serena only rested her hand on the hilt of her sword, instead of drawing it.

"Can you hear them?" she asked. Did she wonder about Ninga's omission about Dr. Emp's powers as well?

Just the edge of the voices reached us. James hurried to pull out a small device from his toolbelt, he stuck a plug in his ear as he mused. "Do you wonder why they all speak English?"

I blinked. "I hadn't, but now I do. What is that?"

His device popped open a small umbrella and he pointed it at them. "Parabolic microphone. Shh."

Serena frowned. "How do they speak English?"

"Shh. Ninga's explaining our quest. Her words. They know and like Miss Fitz."

I stared back at the spear bearers with fierce faces, they hadn't eased. The Oon that Ninga spoke to gave softer glances back to us though.

"I missed part, but someone named Bao can help us." Even as he spoke, a warrior was sent off back to the middle of the domes and disappeared behind them. "We can pass through to the stone flats." He palmed the device guiltily as Ninga turned to return.

I flushed and Serena suddenly found leaves to

study. Ninga seemed not to notice. "We are welcome, but their historian will meet you here at the edge."

"Historian?" I asked.

Ninga cocked her head. "Yes. What surprises you?"

That rabbits had a historian, but I wasn't going to say that. "I hadn't expected it from such a small settlement."

She frowned at my attempt. "Stay here. I'm going to talk with a couple of old friends."

The warriors held their line between us and the domes; not threatening, but ready. Had any of them ever seen Dr. Emp and realized we were similar? Was he human? We had assumed so, based on his appearance and clothes, though they were odd.

James slipped off his pack and began preparing a drone. All of our guards watched him.

An Oon with dark gray fur and cream streaks hobbled toward us with wide eyes. I couldn't tell if his legs hurt him or if he was terrified. He passed the warriors, exchanging quick glances before he rose straighter and approached. "I am Bao, historian of the Biddies."

I kept my face straight. He said the name funnier than I did. "Thank you for helping us."

His nod told me I'd been properly polite. "What would you know?" He frowned at James and his drone.

"Have you seen Dr. Emp's fortress?" Serena asked.

"All can see it." Bao's tone dismissed her question. "If you stand outside the forest."

"Have you seen it up close?"

His eyes widened again and his head pulled back. "Never."

She sagged. "So you wouldn't know if it were difficult to sneak into."

He was starting to shake his head when James's drone whirred and popped up into the air. "What is that?"

"A drone." James showed him the screen. The image was of the settlement dwindling as he flew above us. "Maybe you can help me with what we see."

Bao leaned in, ignoring the buzzing above. "Magic."

"Tech, but sure."

The screen showed the woods stretching out for a long distance straight ahead, but only a short distance to the right where dust and rocks took up the horizon until distant mountains peaked. James flew the drone in that direction. "Are these the stone flats?" he asked.

The historian nodded slowly. "Amazing. Yes. A little to the right." He hesitated as he pointed, unwilling to get too close to us or the screen. "See that dark rise, that is your fortress."

As the drone sped forward, the dust on the ground turned flat and cracked in spots. Rocks still cropped up in places, but we were traveling over stone. On the far right, two Vodynash were jogging.

James kept flying straight, but spun the camera to get a view of them.

All of us stiffened, and Bao stepped back. No one spoke.

When the view turned forward again, the fortress appeared only a bit larger.

"That is a long way to go without being seen," Serena murmured.

The drone slowed and the view spun to the left where the distant forest cut an edge on the horizon. There were dunes along that edge, not flat rock. "Have you been there?" James asked Bao.

The Oon shook his head slowly. "I don't believe so. It does not look familiar." He turned from the screen to study the three of us in turn. "You truly intend to go to the fortress."

Serena straightened. "Yes."

"Then you will die."

I drew in a long breath. "What can you tell of us of Dr. Emp? He can control minds?"

"Yes. He cares for nothing that we know of — only power. None have ever escaped and none have ventured toward his fortress since he enslaved Oon to help build it. There are a couple Mothers who met him when he first wandered our land, so I've heard." Bao closed his eyes. "You will die, or worse."

I swallowed and watched the screen. The drone buzzed toward us with the woods full in view. A clearing just off the edge of the dunes had a collection of broken clay domes. We would have no cover once we left the trees. "How long before night?" I gestured toward the sky.

"Night?" Bao asked.

"After the sun goes down," answered Serena.

"Sun?"

She frowned at the ambient light stretched overhead. "When does the sky turn dark with no light?"

The Oon historian's eyebrows rose and his ears twitched. "Never. That's horrifying."

My heart sank. We were about to approach an evil wizard in a fortress guarded by mind controlled bogeymen in broad daylight, but Bao considered night a disaster. The only other choice we had was to find someplace quiet to live out our lives in this dismal place.

James's drone buzzed over the settlement, drawing Oon heads up.

It was time to leave.

CHAPTER 15
HIDDEN UNDER THE SAND

WE REACHED the edge of the stone flats in less than an hour. Ninga seemed reluctant to step too far beyond the opening from the trail. A faint hint of something burnt clung to the dust we stirred up, and the air felt warmer.

The fortress was a vague, dark lump rising from the lighter gray. There were no more Vodynash running from it, and a scan along the edge of the woods gave no hint of movement.

"How long do you think it will take to walk there?" I asked Ninga.

She shrugged, eyes wide. At her feet was cracked stone that webbed ahead of us, dusted in areas and dotted with pebbles. The ground was different than the hard gray soil in the settlements or around the portal.

James pointed along the line of trees to my left. "If we want to use those dunes to hide our approach, we need to go that way first." I half expected him to pull out another drone, but maybe he was saving his batteries until we were closer.

Serena pivoted sharply and led the way, leaving Ninga dashing to catch up. I studied the fortress as I followed, easily keeping pace. We were walking, not running down trails. The stone scuffed under my feet and an occasional pebble clattered away from an unintentional kick.

James trailed behind us all. "We're going to stand out in dark clothes once we're away from this tree line, but I can't think of anything we can do about it."

I glanced down at my dark T-shirt. It would contrast against the pale gray. "Let's hope they don't keep lookouts. It sounds like they shouldn't expect anyone to approach."

No one spoke, so I asked Ninga a question I doubted she could answer. "How many Vodynash does Dr. Emp have under his control? Ten, or like a hundred?"

Her ears twitched. "I've heard of a group of twelve surrounding a settlement to kidnap Oons. That's the most I've heard of in one place."

I stepped over a larger crack in the stone that appeared deep with shadows turning the bottom black. From the drone video, at least six were in the woods behind us. Maybe there weren't too many and they would be searching the settlements, never expecting us to go right for the fortress. It might have been a hopeless dream, but it made me feel better.

"I'm getting hungry." I plucked my water bottle off the side of my bag. "Before we head into the dunes, let's grab snacks." There were some peanut butter crackers at the bottom of my pack, mainly because they were one of my least favorite. James had Nilla wafers. "What do Oon eat here?" I asked Ninga.

"Sweet grass, white seed when it's in season, low grape," she gestured toward the woods to our left, "and almost all the leaves."

I'd only seen the fat leaves of the trees and the smaller Chia sized ones. Neither sounded tasty; I wasn't big on salad.

"Grape?" asked James as he slowed. He loved fruit.

"Turns your tongue purple," said Ninga.

"Does it taste good?"

"Very."

James glanced back at me and I shrugged. "Serena. Grapes?"

Twisting to glance back at us, she nodded reluctantly. "A quick bite. We should have planned for a dinner."

We should have planned for Vodynash and Taar, but we hadn't thought about this very much at all. As a group we shifted toward the woods, though I couldn't see any grapes, nothing but the same dusty-gray leaves.

Ninga eyes must have been excellent to have seen the tiny dots nestled deep in the leaves. The dark grapes were the size of raisins and hung off gray vines near the bottom.

James plucked one, cocked his head, and ate it.

"Tasty. But we should let me be the test. In case I get sick." His tongue had turned the warned dark purple.

"You won't." My stomach was growling at the sight. The Oon ate them, but they weren't human. He would be fine. I moved down and began picking them. They were packed with juice, despite resembling raisins. Pulling too hard on one, I ended up with purple fingertips.

Ninga popped them in her mouth, climbing deeper into the woods to harvest them.

When we each had a good handful, James had eaten only the one, we juggled them as we dug through our packs coming up with random envelops and Ziplocs to store them in. I retrieved the crackers. "Two each?"

"I've got the Nilla wafers as well." James pulled out the slightly crumpled box.

So, we had a dinner of Nilla wafers and peanut butter crackers at the edge of the woods, staring at the ominous bump in the horizon that was Dr. Emp's fortress. We were no closer, but the dunes rose and fell to our left. It would only take a few minutes to get there.

I pointed at an entrance in the forest close to the dunes. "Another trail."

Ninga spoke from within the woods. "That led out from the Santh settlement. There were many Oon taken from there to build the fortress. A friend, Atat, was among them. Her son and those who survived moved far away."

"I'm sorry," I said. How many of Ninga's friends were at the fortress? She seemed to know everyone.

"It was long ago." Ninga's tone was sad and quiet. She might not expect Atat to have survived.

I ate one more sweet wafer, not wanting to eat all our supplies. Serena stood and shrugged on her pack. It was time to continue and we had no idea if we'd make it very far without being spotted. I didn't like our chances. I imagined us running back here to the woods to hide was more likely than finding Miss Fitz at the fortress. We had to try.

The dunes were not dusty when we stepped into them a few minutes later. My foot sank in the speckled sand like on an ocean beach. "This is going to be hard to walk in."

"Probably why the Vodynash use the stone." Serena led us again, plodding with a slight tilt forward.

Some of the cracks I'd seen made me think I'd break an ankle if I had to run across the stone flats. The Vodynash looked tougher than I was. We started up the first rise that hid the fortress and horizon. Each step slid sand down and left little forward progress. At the top, the stone flats were easily visible. "Anyone could see us."

Ninga handled the dunes easier than me and James, keeping up with Serena on the next incline. We hadn't forced the Oon to join us, but I felt a little guilt anyway. We might all be making a big mistake.

Each trip down, James and I would catch up a little, but Serena and Ninga were still a few paces ahead when they entered a bottom between two dunes. I was thinking about how those grapes might taste. James hadn't gotten sick.

A long thin line of sand burst into the air to the right of Serena, and a second much farther to the left. Moving so swiftly that I could hardly focus on the shape, a long gray tentacle whipped out of the spray of sand and slapped onto her.

She might have leaped free, if it weren't for the soft footing. Lurching to the side, she still couldn't avoid the finger-thick cord winding around her once, then twice. The other tentacle smacked the sand where Ninga had been, but the Oon had danced out of the way. Something, or some things, were hidden under the sand.

Without knowing what I was going to do, I raced forward.

CHAPTER 16
TIME FOR A NAP

JAMES STAYED CLOSE BEHIND ME, I could hear him huffing. Ninga sprang from one place to the next, avoiding the tentacle that searched for her. It wasn't puckered like an octopus, more like a very active vine.

Serena was pulled to the sand, arms pinned against her side and feet kicking. The tentacle that had her in a firm grip had receded into the dune as if to drag her with it. Before we reached her, it started shifting her body back and forth until her left arm had disappeared into the ground.

"Cut it," she yelled. Her Athame and sword hilt were held under the wraps, and I had no blade.

"James, you must have a knife." Staff ready, I knew my slash spell was too wild to risk. I might cut Serena open instead of the tentacle. With all the tools he carried, there had to be a Swiss Army knife. I spun when a whirring sounded behind me.

James held a device that had a small handle with

a spinning blur at the end, maybe two-inches in diameter, like a mini weed-whacker. "Hold onto her feet and pull. Don't let it drag her under." He dove to his knees beside her.

My heart was racing but I dropped my staff and grabbed her boots. In my mind, I imagined pulling her free.

James shook his head as he brought the whirring blade to the edge of a tentacle and began to cut. The air smelled like apple pie for a second as an opening split the tentacle where he touched.

Whatever creature lay beneath the sands whipped loose from Serena, slapping into James. His device tumbled onto the dune as he grunted.

As I had imagined, Serena lurched free in my hands. I went down on my butt and she sprang up, blades in her grasp.

The other tentacle chasing Ninga withdrew and I was the only one sprawled out on their back.

"What was that thing?" Serena's sharp tone rang out in the quiet of the dunes.

Ninga snapped her head to respond, but her eyes were on the ground. "I do not know."

James retrieved his device warily. "I think it was a plant. No blood and it looked like wood inside of bark."

Grabbing my staff, I managed to scuffle to my feet. "Maybe that's why everyone sticks to the stone."

Serena jabbed the tip of her sword into the sand where the tentacle holding her had withdrawn. "I'm going to cut it clean off if it tries it again."

"Let's get up to the ridge." Jamming my staff into the dune, I plodded up the slope. "They might live – or grow at the bottoms, whatever they are." I had a vision of a tangle of vines under the sand, waiting to drag us down to whatever roots it had.

After one last jab, Serena scampered up, passing me.

My heart was thudding. Vodynash and whatever hid in the sands were what we had to deal with, and that was before we reached Dr. Emp and his mind control.

Serena glared at me when I didn't follow. "We're not leaving without Miss Fitz and the Dewi Sri."

What if Miss Fitz had returned to her classroom? I considered suggesting that I head back to the portal with Ninga to see if she could open it for us. That would just split us up, and I couldn't take the chance that Miss Fitz would be left to some horrible fate.

I rolled my eyes and trudged toward Serena. "We'll find Miss Fitz."

We navigated the next drop in the dunes carefully, keeping to a slope on the side rather than traipsing through the middle. I kept my staff ready. I'd use the slash spell even though it wasn't one of my best. Serena had her sword tip pointed at the ground, and James kept his device in hand.

Nothing whipped out at us. It became almost embarrassing to keep expecting more tentacles or vines. I eased enough to drink some water, but Serena kept her blades ready. She'd seemed more angry than terrified like I was. Despite the recent excitement, my eyes were starting to get dry and tired.

To our left, a dark shadow cut through the sand, hidden in spots where the dunes rose higher. I noticed and paused at the next rise. "There's a canyon or something over there." The edge of a cliff showed dark-gray rock exposed under sloping sand.

James craned to get a view. "Definitely."

I turned and studied the dunes ahead. "Let's hope it doesn't cut us off ahead." From what I could tell, the ravine ran parallel to us aiming for the fortress ahead. It was shaped clearly like a cube, not a fancy castle like I'd imagined. There was a stubby tower rising out of the middle, but none of the shades of gray gave a hint of windows. I could make out lines that suggested layers of stone blocks. "It doesn't look like much."

He huffed and dug at the side of his tool belt. "I wonder if I should send up a drone. I don't want to burn up all my batteries." James pulled out a short tube that turned out to be a telescope as it whirred when he looked through it.

Serena paused, already descending. "What do you see?"

"Stone building. There are only a couple slits for windows. An entrance facing that way." He jabbed a thumb to the right. There's a smaller structure on the top that might be two stories, so I'd say the whole thing is six stories tall. No guards on the roof or outside watching the door." He passed the telescope to me.

I scanned over the fortress he described, somewhat disappointed and relieved. It could have been abandoned for the lack of activity. "Maybe all the Vodynash are searching for us." Our luck hadn't been great, so I didn't count on it.

Ninga's ears perked at my comment. She'd been quiet since her encounter.

James walked beside me. "We might want to rest when we get to the fortress. Miss Fitz says our magic is strongest after a sleep."

"If the Vodynash are all out searching for us, it might be the only opportunity we have."

He nodded. "There's Dr. Emp. What do we do about him?"

I'd been thinking about his mind control. "Stun. All of us."

"Then?"

That had been as far as I'd gotten, but I had thoughts. "Knock him unconscious."

James frowned. "That's tricky. A blow to the head might kill, or do nothing. It's not as easy as they make it look in the movies."

Heat flushed up my cheeks. "What do you suggest?"

"I wish I had something. We didn't grab any potions to make someone sleep, I know Vera's Paste works well if taken swallowed."

I glanced at Serena's backpack. She'd packed mainly healing potions and some explosives. "Maybe Serena has an idea." Surely with her martial arts she'd learned to knock someone out.

He made a slashing motion with his hand. "Her solution might be more permanent than I'm willing to go."

"She wouldn't kill someone. At least not unless they were trying to kill her. She'd disable them." I spoke quietly even though she was a few paces ahead of us climbing the next rise. "A short rest might be good." My legs were sore from all our walking and the sand made it worse.

"A tactical nap," James agreed.

"What's that?"

"Some say as little as eight minutes, others twenty." He smiled. "YouTube."

My legs, tilting into the next soft incline, agreed wholeheartedly. Just the thought of it made me yawn. I dug into my pocket and pulled out my cell phone. "It's almost midnight."

"On our world."

I peered up at the dull sky. "Never night here."

Ahead of us, at the top of the rise, Serena dropped to the sand. "Vodynash."

I had nearly reached the crest and knelt, scanning the horizon ahead. Two distant gray shapes jogged out along the dunes with the fortress rising behind them. I panicked. "They spotted us."

It only took a second to determine my mistake. They'd be passing to our right, very close though. Any thought of being tired vanished as my pulse raced.

CHAPTER 17
ONE NASTY PROBLEM AT A TIME

"WE NEED TO GO THAT WAY." I pointed, then saw the darker shadow of the canyon. "As far as we can."

"I can put a drone on the top of a dune and monitor their progress." James settled beside me, telescope to his eye. "They're ugly."

Ninga snorted, and we all glanced at her. "Sorry," she said. What did she think of us?

We were close enough to the fortress to make it out clearly. There were bigger buildings in Tallahassee, but to the inhabitants of the Gray Domain, it was probably impressive.

Serena crawled backward. "Let's move. I don't want them seeing us."

We had to take a twisting route to keep from climbing one of the rises. When it became inevitable without a long trip back toward the woods, I stopped us. "Probably a good time for a drone," I said to James. Serena nodded.

Ninga's ears dropped back, but she just kept an eye back where we expected the Vodynash to be traveling. We didn't need them topping a rise and seeing us.

As James slid off his backpack, I pointed to a crest in the direction we'd been trying to go. "If we can tell when they're going down to a bottom, then we can climb that quickly and get to the other side. We're going to have to wait at some point, but I'd like it to be farther away."

He nodded, then his lips tightened. "What if they find our tracks?"

I groaned inside, not wanting to imagine that. "One nasty problem at a time."

He fired up the drone and it rose slowly scanning in the direction we had last seen the Vodynash. They were jogging up a slope, but moving slow through the sand. "Higher." I needed to see how steep the next slope dropped.

James sucked air through his teeth and Serena tilted her head, but our view rose.

"This is our chance." I started for the incline. "We need to time it so we're over the top when they're at the bottom."

"Or we wait here until they pass."

They would come too close. I glanced back toward the direction we'd come. If I could see those rises, then someone atop them could see us. "I vote we move."

James and Serena nodded. We spread out and began to crawl up the sand slowly, waiting for a word from him. "Go."

I didn't look back. James watched his screen in one hand while he climbed. If the Vodynash spotted us and began running toward us, we'd have to make some quick choices. The last few steps to the top of the rise I held my breath. Serena toppled down the far side, regardless of the sand spraying. Ninga was next, followed by James and me.

"Well?" Serena asked James.

"They never saw us."

We lay panting on the slope as James drifted the drone back to us. The ravine was close, only a few dunes away. I was curious, so when the drone flew toward the shadow, I crawled over beside James.

It wasn't deep. Sand filled it. There were a few walls of rock visible a story or two high, but in other areas the dune just spilled into it. "We could walk down there."

"If there's no tentacle vines," he said.

The drone lifted and turned to face Dr. Emp's fortress. The canyon, a shallow groove in the dunes really, merged with the sand only a short walk from here. "It'll keep the Vodynash from seeing us. I'd risk it." I peered across to the next rise, and already plotted a windy path between us and the ravine.

Serena, listening to us a few feet away, nodded and scrambled down, sword pointed toward the sand.

We reached the ravine, a bit more imposing as we stepped and half slid down a long slope to the bottom. James recalled his drone, packed it, and we climbed in.

The top of the fortress remained in sight as we walked. We stopped to bring out our grapes. They weren't as sweet as I hoped, but they tasted good.

Ninga refused those we offered. "Thank you, but I ate plenty." Her tongue and lips were still purple.

When Serena spoke, I stifled a laugh at her colored lips. "Do we go in the front door?"

"I hope we can find something more subtle." James smirked at my mouth as I popped another grape into it. "I think I should run another drone around the building to look for a better way in."

By the time we reached the end of the ravine where the sand formed one last ramp, we found the Vodynash behind us making for the woods. I hoped they didn't happen upon our tracks. The fortress appeared a little more foreboding, but at this vantage point we could only see the one wall and the top of the tower. The windows were dark slits, scattered randomly; a total of eight by my count.

"Drone?" asked Serena.

"I'm going to wait until we're a little closer. I've got a strong signal, but I still have range limitations and I'd hate to lose connection on the far side of the building." James smiled apologetically, but we'd have little options without his tech. We might have lost Serena to the tentacle vines without it.

I was watching the building as he spoke and stopped dead when a motion flickered at the roof. "There's someone there."

As a group, we dropped to the ground, but we were dark shapes on the pale sand.

At the top edge of the building, a black silhouette came into focus, framed against the light gray sky. It was likely a Vodynash, or else Dr. Emp had taken off his hat. The figure walked to the corner, paused perhaps to search the dunes, then turned sideways to us and walked the edge of the building. "It is guarded," I said.

"Let's just hope they don't find four dots in the sand something worth investigating." James had his head down, peering up.

The guard paused about a third of the way along the side, almost directly ahead. Then he turned and faced our direction.

My breath hitched, and I stared motionless, fighting down a desire to run. "They're going to see us."

"We can't do anything but wait," Serena whispered. It wasn't like they could hear our voices.

It took forever before the guard continued on their path, pausing partway down, but still not reacting in alarm.

"What if they did see us?" said James. "But are acting like they don't."

"A trap?" I asked. It took everything not to check behind us.

"I don't think they're that smart." Serena still kept her voice low.

It took a few minutes before the sentry reached the left corner, turned, and disappeared walking away. Serena was up in second. "Hurry. We need to reach the wall before they make a lap." She took off with Ninga close behind her.

If my thighs and calves had complained about walking in the soft sand, they screamed at running, but I kept up. James had it worse with his heavy pack. The windows grew larger, sure to betray us. The stone blocks were bigger than I imagined the Oon could move, but someone had built Dr. Emp's fortress.

I almost laughed when the sand gave way to stone beneath our feet. Ahead was flat rock. My legs ached, but we reached the fortress. I shook as we pressed our backs against the wall and studied the dunes behind us. The woods were a thin edge on the horizon, but there were no Vodynash following. We all took a moment to catch our breath.

"Now we find a way inside." Serena studied the top of the building, then the front of the building to my left where the entrance lay.

My relief faded and I tilted my head back, peering up the stone wall to a distant sky. I didn't really want to be trapped inside with a wizard who could control minds.

"I'm sending a drone around the back and other side to scout for an opening." James dropped to his knees, sliding out of his backpack. "I'm running low on batteries, but I've been swapping out partially drained ones."

I dropped to sit against the wall, giving my legs a moment and grabbing my water. Ninga paced along the side, and soon Serena joined her, both glancing up. Somewhere above us a sentry walked, though I didn't hear him.

The drone whirred into life, sounding loud enough to make me grimace. It shot off low to the ground toward the back corner. It hung there and I turned my attention to the screen. James and I both leaned in as the view eased around the corner.

The first opening to catch our interest was about a story high and round with sediment crusting the edges. More crusted debris covered the ground below except for where a wide grate covered a massive hole. As he crept the drone forward, I could see the circumference was almost twice my height and muck covered the wooden grating.

The second shape was a dark rectangle that marked a door about halfway down the fortress. The drone crawled forward until it was an obvious door made of wood boards. The hinges appeared to be made of leather rather than metal and a cord hung from a hole beside a wooden handle.

"Well, we found a way in." James passed the door with a quick burst from the drone.

"What's that?" I pointed to a low wall far behind the fortress at the left edge of his screen.

He pivoted and the clay edges of an Oon well were obvious almost twenty paces from the doorway. Grass grew around the edge, the only sign of life we'd seen on these stone flats.

James continued, slowing the drone to a near stop at the far corner. The opposite side of the building was like ours, empty except for window slits higher up. As he brought the drone back, I stood to join Serena who had stopped her pacing to watch.

"I'll go first," I offered. "Everyone else hang back in case we need to run."

Serena scoffed. "Good plan, except I'm the only one of us who can fend off a close combat attack. I go first, you hang back." She raised her sword and I didn't argue.

In a couple of minutes we hung near the corner, and James had aimed his listening device at the door. The reek from the pit made me want to gag; it was worse than the potion Chet had put in my hair.

"I don't hear any voices or noises, but that doesn't mean anything." James tucked the device in a vest pocket.

While Serena crept up to the door circumventing the drainage hole, we kept within view in case we needed to cast spells in her defense. She'd put away her Athame so she had a hand free to open the door. We could be walking into the Vodynash barracks, for all we knew.

My pulse pounded in my ears, but I had my staff ready in front of me, as did James. We both grimaced when she skirted the edge of the wooden grate.

When she was two steps away from the door, it opened.

CHAPTER 18
DRABS

A THIN OON stepped out of the door with a lopsided clay pot in their hands. Their face was slack without any expression. Ahead of me and James, Serena froze.

The Oon walked slowly with none of the usual spring I'd seen from Ninga or the others. Their head never moved to indicate they'd seen Serena. I shivered as they plodded toward the well as if in a trance. If this was Dr. Emp's mind control, it scared me more now than what my imagination had come up with.

Serena only took a short pause before padding to the door and peering inside. With one glance back to the Oon, she waved us forward.

I held my breath, more because of the stench of the pit than out of apprehension, and crept toward her. Ninga and James followed me.

The door was more ragged than I'd assumed when the drone had passed by. The leather hinges let it hang at a tilt and the cord obviously worked a thin wooden latch. The frame was rough-hewn and appeared crooked. Serena waited until we were almost to the doorway before stepping inside and out of sight. It was probably not a Vodynash barracks then.

The blocks were not even, leaving gaps in the frame. The floor was rock and mortar with no hint of being polished flat.

Serena stood in a hall with walls and ceiling made of rough wood planks, with larger timbers supporting a corner where the corridor intersected another. There were Oon voices from somewhere deeper inside the rough castle; she pulled back a woven drape to peer into a dark room to my left. I'd seen pictures and movies of fortresses and this looked like I tried to build it with an ax and hammer. James would have done better, but he had his dad's cool tools.

We clustered in the hall, and while Serena crept toward the intersection, I nervously watched the Oon drawing up a bucket of water outside. I imagined them zombified enough to walk right back in past us without a word.

Serena sniffed and pointed to the woven door as she tiptoed toward us. I could hear footsteps scuffling on stone from the other hall.

Ninga darted into the tiny room with James following behind. With little light, I could see shelves before the flap closed, then a last glimpse of a rather large pantry before Serena entered, remaining at the doorway, drape closed. The scent of something nutty hung in the air. In the darkness, I dared not move around in case I kicked a basket or crate. Someone walked on the floor above. How many Oon were in the castle?

With only distant sounds of activity above and around us, I closed my eyes. We had never taken a nap, not with a sentry walking the walls above. I'd hate to be caught snoring when they came in for supplies.

Serena shifted, whispering to us. "We should wait until the Oon getting water comes back in, then I'll scout."

James snorted quietly. "I don't know that they'd even notice you."

"Want to take that chance?" Her tone was sharp, though she kept her voice low.

"No."

Ninga spoke in the darkness to my side. "I should be the one to scout."

I cocked my head, but didn't voice my agreement. We humans might cause a stir walking into a group of Oon, but in their state, they might not think anything about another one of their own kind. We had no plan, but if Ninga could get a glimpse at our surroundings, we might come up with one.

Serena must have felt the same, as she agreed after a long pause. "Okay. Once they close the back door."

I'd opened my eyes, and the woven flap leaked some light through it, and there was less than an inch at the bottom where the sky peeking from the open back-door lit the stone floor. I could make out Serena's hair and a glint off her sword. James was to my right but hidden in darkness deeper in the pantry. Something smelled edible, but it wouldn't do to forage blindly.

It took forever for the Oon to return, close the door, and amble down the hall. Serena eventually pulled the drape back to peek, then motioned Ninga out. Even as our guide shifted into the hall, we gathered at the flap to listen. Mixed with an occasional thud or clack, there was still the distant murmur of a couple of Oon speaking. I felt trapped, but grateful there was a door nearby. I winced when I thought of going up higher in the building.

The Oon talking grew excited, and my heart dropped. They'd surely found Ninga.

Serena gave me a fierce glance, lowering the flap to the width of a finger, but still able to peer out. When no alarm or shouting came, our breathing relaxed.

James whispered from lower down. "That's Ninga talking. She's explaining about us." He had his listening device poked into the hall.

Whatever momentary ease I'd found vaporized. "She's betraying us?"

"Hmm, more like a simple description of what we're doing. Oh." He stopped, leaving me hanging in silence.

"What?" I tried to keep frustration from raising my voice.

"They're on their way here." He stepped away from the door.

Indeed, the Oon voices were getting louder. We shuffled back and one of the others bumped a crate. I didn't want to believe Ninga would turn us in to Dr. Emp's people. There was no cry of alarm and no thudding of heavy Vodynash feet, but I couldn't keep the panic from climbing into my throat. As they turned the corner, I considered bursting out and making for the back door.

"So, there's been no sign of Miss Fitz?" Ninga asked.

"Never here at the castle. They brought in more Oon two days ago, that's been the only change beyond the alarms this morning. I counted eight Vodynash guards heading out." The other Oon's voice was female and she sounded tired, perhaps sad.

"How is your son?" Ninga's voice dropped gently into a consoling tone.

There was a pause, though their steps brought them near to the flap. "The same. He is upstairs, cleaning the barracks."

"My condolences. I am glad to see that you are not — affected too badly." Ninga's hand grasped the edge of the flap and pulled so she could peek in. "There is a friend, Sen, who you should meet. She has news about your search for Miss Fitz."

I'd heard that Miss Fitz was not here, but that didn't help us if we were trapped in the Gray Domain. We could continue searching for her among the settlements, amid the Vodynash, Taar, and spear-tossing Oon.

Ninga stepped in followed by a similar looking Oon, though with paler hair and much thinner; Sen carried a small lamp. She pushed it into the room ahead of herself and studied us under its pale-yellow glow. "Oh, my. They are small. Are they young?" Her eyes were bright, unlike the Oon fetching water.

Serena held her sword ready. "How do you know Miss Fitz?

Sen let the flap drop behind her. "She has been coming to the Gray Domain since before I was born. I'd been raised to Mother of — of my settlement before we were captured. Miss Fitz probably met me when I was hopping on all fours in my family's yute. I remember her coming by as I grew older. She is not here. Who is she to you?"

"We're her students," I said. Part of me wanted to know what a "yute" was, but we had to make a decision. "We came to rescue her."

"And to get the Dewi Sri," added Serena. Her face was shadowed from the small lamp giving her an angry expression.

"Well, I have not seen her, or even know what a Dewi Sri is. The Master has only two places he might hold someone. The first is the cell inside the Vodynash barracks on the second floor, and I was up there earlier and there was no — one being held there." She shivered slightly. "The other location is on the fourth floor where the Master adjusts minds. I know there are two new Oon manacled there, but no one else. I am sorry, but Miss Fitz is not here. You should leave. You're only children, of that I am sure."

I stiffened at the comment, not that she wasn't right about our ages, but that we were to be dismissed so easily because of it. "We killed a Taar." My skin warmed at the boast.

She glanced at Ninga, who nodded, but she shook her head. "The Master is worse than a Taar, and he has six Vodynash left here in the castle. He could give the word and all of us, even myself with only a touch of his control or those deadened with his control, would hunt you down."

I remembered the dull Oon collecting water. Sen was different, but still claimed to be under Dr. Emp's sway.

"We should leave and see if Miss Fitz is out in one of the settlements." James spoke quietly, which reminded me that I'd been loud.

Serena stiffened. "Even if she isn't here, we should retrieve the Dewi Sri. Then we can go search for her." She argued with James, ignoring the Oon.

He didn't reply but turned to me instead.

My eyebrows arched. "I'm not in charge."

"Of course not. But what do you think?" Serena's tone was a challenge.

I'd begun to wish kwe'd waited at the classroom for Miss Fitz, but I couldn't blame that on anyone but me. I didn't entirely trust Ninga's friend, and maybe not even Ninga. However, climbing up four levels, to make sure she wasn't lying about Miss Fitz, intimidated me. "How difficult would it be to get up to the fourth floor?" I studied Sen, wondering if I could tell if she would betray us. "Would he keep a small statue there?"

"The drabs will pay no attention to you, but if you cross a stray Vodynash it won't go well. Master keeps his collections on the fourth floor, you might find your object there, but you might also find him. Wukad is usually with him."

"Wukad?" Serena asked. "Who's that?"

"The only Oon who willingly follows the Master. He has advised him since the beginning." Sen's tone touched on anger and her eyes narrowed. Her expression alone had me trusting her.

"Can you lead us up there?" My hope was she would not betray us. At least warn us if a Vodynash walked a corridor. Plus, check to see if Dr. Emp and this Wukad were in the room when we searched for the Dewi Sri. I flashed her a hopeful smile.

We were a small circle of lamplit faces in a room full of shadows. James sighed and scratched his head. He would go with Serena and I. Ninga closed her eyes as if resigned to help us. We would all be in danger.

Sen sighed and nodded. "If you must go."

"We do."

CHAPTER 19
THE FOURTH FLOOR

I PUSHED past them all through the drape and stepped into the hall. Serena gave me a sharp glance as I did so, though Ninga and her friend trotted out without a thought. My lips tightened as I followed too close behind the Oon. Despite Serena's protests that I wasn't in charge, I felt like the decision had been mine.

She tugged at my elbow, drawing me back. "Let them check the hall."

I couldn't stop her from diving in with her sword if we came upon a Vodynash. "This is my fault." My eyebrows rose; I hadn't expected to admit it.

Serena snorted, lightly. "You didn't make me come." She fell in on my right side with both blades ready.

"I shouldn't have jumped through the portal behind Ninga."

"We were packed and ready to go, what did you think we were going to do?"

I frowned and fell silent. The Oons had reached the corner and strode to the right without a pause. Serena and I reached the cross corridor and peered in both directions. To the left, the hall went down about ten yards before opening up into a large room with just the ends of tables visible and cabinets lining the back wall.

Ninga and Sen led the other direction where doorways dotted every few yards on one side or the other until the passageway ended. There was no one to be seen, though I still heard footsteps on the floor above. Heavy ones that had me imagining bulky Vodynash.

"Shouldn't there be stairs?" James walked a pace back to my left, his wand in hand, but not telescoped out.

"Has to be," I said. Maybe ladders considering the construction of the building. We were passing the first dark room and Sen's lamp barely lit the covering drape in the wide hall. I thought we were walking close to the middle of the fortress, though I couldn't be sure. It smelled faintly of the locker room at school.

"There wouldn't be anyone upstairs if there weren't," Serena mumbled.

Our Oon escorts were about four paces ahead and we kept to their speed so we didn't catch up to them. The rough wooden wall bulged just past the door, as if constructed badly. Even without his father's tools, James would have done better. I grimaced and focused on the danger that lay ahead, not the shabby woodwork.

The hairs on my neck bristled and I slowed my step, glancing furtively about. At the far end behind us, there was no one in the big room.

Ahead, a heavy door creaked open and a drape covering a door shook with a breeze. Dim light lit the doorway and Sen hissed, stopping to wave us back.

James dove for the flap we'd just passed, darting inside with me close on his heels. Serena paused, crouched like a leopard, as if she might fight. The room appeared to be empty, unused storage.

I pressed against the wall beside the door as she backed in. Ninga and Sen stood peering down the hall. The flap closed behind Serena and I didn't dare pull it back to peek.

Heavy footsteps slapped on the stone. "Vodynash," James whispered.

A heavy slam carried as they closed a door. Feet thumping on wood slowly turned into the unmistakable thuds of two of the creatures climbing wooden stairs, even accompanied by an occasional creak. My own pulse competed in my ears as the heavy footfalls grew more distant, eventually stepping onto the floor above us. Dull grunts were muffled on the next floor.

"We're clear." Serena pulled open the drape.

Indeed, Ninga peered back at us, silhouetted by the lamp Sen held.

My neck prickled again. "Wait."

She frowned at me, but stopped. "Why?"

I drew in a deep breath, flushing as I felt foolish.

"I —"What could I say? Something told me not to go into the hall.

The Vodynash were still walking about upstairs, then my chest tightened when I recognized their feet on steps again. A pair were coming down, grumbling between themselves.

Serena let the flap drop closed.

"Shift change?" James asked in a hoarse, quiet voice. "Maybe they're taking turns searching for us."

It had been hours since we arrived. If the two Vodynash went out the heavy door, then James was likely right.

Instead, their heavy feet slapped into the hall setting my heart in my throat.

"Move," one growled outside our door.

"Hungry," a second Vodynash said in a deep grumble.

I expected them to whip open the drape and find us trapped in this room. Their heavy feet trod past our door and the flimsy wall at my back rocked. My breath sounded too loud.

They stomped down the hall toward the large room at the opposite end of the hall and began barking out orders for food. I tried not to think about it too much, but my pulse was slowing. They weren't searching for us in the fortress, not yet.

It was an agonizing five minutes before they returned and went out the front door as James had predicted. None of us spoke until the heavy door slammed shut behind them.

"How do we understand them?" asked James.

"How did you know?" Serena spoke to me in a quiet tone.

I blinked, pondering both their questions. Touching the back of my neck, I answered Serena. "It was a feeling, like something bad was going to happen, but it didn't." Shrugging it off, I pushed aside the curtain, stuck my head out and peered in both directions.

Ninga sagged against the wall, obviously distressed. Sen held her hand, comforting her. I hadn't even considered what they'd been going through in the hall.

"I'm sorry, Ninga." My voice was low, barely a whisper, but her ears flicked.

She straightened. "Thank you. I'll be fine. Luckily they didn't find you."

Serena and James arrayed beside me. He arrived to hear her response and hadn't seen her shaken. "How do we understand you? Surely not everyone here speaks English."

Ninga shook her head. "I don't know the word, but the portal has that effect. I could understand the Vodynash." She nodded to the other Oon. "I imagine Sen can't."

"Snarls is all. But we get the idea soon enough. Food or water." Sen shivered. "Let's get past the second floor." She trotted down the hall with Ninga joining her, and we followed cautiously behind.

"We know where the stairs are now," I whispered to James.

The Oons reached the flap and stood holding it open for us so we had some light from Sen's lamp. The room beyond had a dim glow creeping in around the frame, though there were no windows. A huge empty chamber, bigger than the largest room at any of our houses except maybe James's garage, there was only one hanging for decoration beside two thick doors.

Someone had painted Dr. Emp on a woven mat. It was more like a cartoon than anything else. The red-orange hat and white feather stood out, as did the long jacket. His chin stuck out too far and his mustache was two thick spikes. He held a book as if reading it.

"That's disturbing," I said.

Serena frowned, barely glancing at it. Her head tilted to study the wide stair that led up on the wall bordering the hall. Ninga was close behind her friend, already on the first step.

I stiffened as the second step creaked. Ninga motioned for us to wait at the base. A window would have been nice as the lamp climbed with them, leaving us in dwindling light.

"Let's hope another pair doesn't come back," James said.

My head whipped toward the door, suddenly horrified. "Yeah. That would be bad."

Serena faced the exit, but her head craned to watch the Oons. I almost wanted to go back in the hall rather than stand in the entryway.

The creaking steps were getting on my nerves.

Somewhere up there Vodynash spoke in muffled voices.

"C'mon." Serena headed for the stairs.

Both relieved to get away from the front door and slightly terrified, I followed her with James at my heels. The landing above had the wall to my left, but on the right side there wasn't even a railing. The voices grew louder. "Snarls," Sen had called the noises. We were heading right to them.

My eyes rolled in my head every time I found a creaking step. Another set of stairs blocked much of the right side, but near the top I could make out a room over the entryway to the right. There were mattresses atop wooden boxes against the outer stone wall. A high thin window let in some light. The foul, pungent scent that wafted through the air reminded me of the zoo.

The wall between us and the voices gave me no glimpse of where the Vodynash were, but they were close. The one door nearest us led into a hall back toward the end where the drab Oon worked in the kitchen.

Ninga and Sen had already climbed the adjacent stairs three-quarters of the way to the third level. I didn't hesitate at the landing, but caught a glimpse of the jail cell they'd mentioned earlier. Dark and empty, a metal gate stood ajar beside iron bars. Miss Fitz wasn't here, and I couldn't know if she cared about the Dewi Sri statue as much as Serena did.

On the third level landing, James spoke. "I don't relish the idea of coming back down."

"Me neither," I said. I wanted to argue for just leaving now.

The stairwell split off to front and back with only a hint of corridor walls behind uncovered openings. Worse, at the top of the stairs leading to the fourth floor, Ninga and Sen stood waiting for us.

There was a door there, not quite as rickety as the back one we'd entered through. Before Sen opened it, she motioned for us to wait.

As she disappeared from view, my trust wavered. Sen could have betrayed us all on the first floor though. Serena's eyes squinted, watching the top intently. James breathed quietly behind me.

Ninga exhaled. "Come." Silently, she disappeared through the doorway.

Serena was the first to enter, and I followed a step behind. Where the rest of the building appeared to have been made of leftover planks, the massive room of the fourth floor had polished walls dotted with proper doors. The wood cabinets alternated with stone wall where the window slits appeared.

James pointed to our right at an odd horizontal window that glimpsed the gray horizon. "That's the front of the building." His voice echoed slightly, and we both cringed.

The staircase was wrapped in the polished wood, standing nearly in the center of the room. Ninga and Sen stood nervously toward the middle. I couldn't see the other corner for the stairwell. Serena, however, had moved closer to the Oons, and stared with wide eyes.

Stepping quietly on the polished floor, I slipped past the corner of the walled-in staircase to join Serena, leaving James to study the window.

In the center of the room, a black spiral staircase wove up into the ceiling. At its base circled a low raised platform. Sitting sideways to us, and oblivious, was an Oon chained to a metal pole that was part of the supports for the steps. My heart wrenched, remembering that two of the Oon were here to have their minds "adjusted." I shivered at the thought.

Those manacles were attached to poles spaced about five feet apart on the platform. I could make out six on this side. Between them were intricately carved shelves braced against the steps. Crowded with objects including books, they reminded me of Miss Fitz's library office.

Outside of the Oon awaiting Dr. Emp's mind manipulation, or perhaps already enthralled, the room that took up the entire floor appeared empty. "Is he upstairs?" I asked Sen.

She nodded and was barely audible. "Most likely."

The wardrobes or storage rooms tucked against the wall took up little space, but there was one odd, larger one protruding out. I pointed to it. "Or in there? What is that?"

"Waste chute. He won't be in there."

Serena had begun stalking forward, eyes riveted on the podium and spiral staircase. "There it is."

As she passed, Sen raised a hand as if to hold her back. "Don't."

Serena had seen the Dewi Sri, surely. I hurried to join her. "Be careful. What if he warded it?" I searched the shelves for the figurine. Miss Fitz had warned us about warding, but we hadn't been taught anything. "Too young," she'd said.

"We didn't come all this way for nothing." Serena nearly growled.

We had. I'd been concerned about Miss Fitz, not her statue, magical or not. She wasn't here or threatened by Dr. Emp in any way I could see. If retrieving the Dewi Sri meant we could leave, then I was all for it.

It sat on a shelf of its own.

I stepped ahead of Serena. "Let me get it — in case it's warded."

CHAPTER 20
DARK CONFINES

I CLIMBED THE SHORT RISE, careful not to let my staff clack on the wood. The winding staircase rose into a windowed room above with more polished wood. There had been a small tower on the top of the fortress and I imagined Dr. Emp had a nice apartment up there from the looks of it.

The scratched, wooden stage had a minty scent that surprised me. Scrapes marred the metal poles where his prisoners had been left. The dark chains and manacles with bolts screwed through them made me shiver.

"Be careful," Serena whispered from behind me. "Be quiet."

I was being *very* quiet. Everyone stood motionless where they'd been before I started for the statue. Ninga appeared horrified.

The Dewi Sri rested eye level on the shelf, so I rose on my toes, searching for runes or sigils marked around it. Up close, the dark brown shelves weren't as polished as they'd seemed, but still better than the rough wood downstairs. Sparkling in what little light there was in the room, the Dewi Sri woman appeared to study me as I did her.

"Safe?" I asked her.

Lips twitching, I lifted the figure off the shelf, pausing for only a moment. I didn't explode. There were no alarms ringing. In truth, I had no idea what to expect of a ward, but knew they existed.

"Safe," I said to myself. Turning with a smile, I found Serena just where I'd left her with her eyes squinting as she studied me and the platform.

Creeping quietly, I made for the edge. James stood closest to the stairs, seeming unwilling to be too close to the podium. He was the smartest of us.

Ninga and Sen didn't appear to breath, but their eyes followed me. Had Sen spent time on the platform, even as little manipulated as she was? Could we free the Oon safely, or would they raise an alarm?

Serena might agree to an attempted rescue.

I glanced at James, who might be more cautious. He took a step back. His eyes were growing wide as he stared above me to the top of the stairs.

Too late, I spun as a high-pitched Oon voice called out in alarm, "Master!"

The spiked shoulders of the woman jabbed into my palm as I tensed. The near-white Oon crouched at the top of the stairwell at a railing. He appeared more rabbit than the others in that position. His beady eyes were locked on me.

"They are here." The Oon, Wakud I guessed, whipped its head back to look deeper in the room.

I didn't wait for his master, Dr. Emp, and leaped off the stage toward Serena.

Ninga and Sen were already running, but not toward James and the stairs. They headed toward the door to what they'd called the waste chute. Serena waited for me, but noted their direction and turned for it.

James appeared torn, between following our guides, who I hoped had a plan, and heading for the stairs. I didn't want us to separate. His feet shifted, but he hadn't moved.

I hit the floor in front of Serena running after Ninga. "C'mon," I yelled at James, pointing toward the fleeing Oon.

Wakud was squealing about the Dewi Sri, but called her the lady. I had no doubt Dr. Emp would be running after us with his ability to control our minds. That did not sound like something we should wait around for.

Serena raced past me as the Oons threw open the door. Sen, followed close by Ninga, jumped into an Oon sized tube that rose from the floor. Stifling images of a video game, I began to question their idea of escape.

"Where does that go?" I asked.

Without answering, Serena bolted for the room. Despite all her bluster about swords, she wasn't stupid when it came to facing magic.

Gratefully, James had decided to join us. He was a

dozen paces behind us, but headed for the open door.

Serena gracefully leaped to the edge, gave me a sharp glance before sheathing her weapons, and dropped in feet first. I could hear her swish down.

I faltered slightly. Small dark places weren't my first choice, and Sen had left her lantern in the room. Flames inside the tube might not be smart either. Just inside the door, the metal stairs clanged with boots.

"Stop," Dr. Emp said. Though I first heard it as a word, his command echoed in my mind.

My feet stumbled, and I tripped to the edge of the tube. It stunk of rot and worse. Part of me was becoming frantic, because I believed I should stop and wait for Dr. Emp. The word repeated inside my brain, nearly the only thought. I could see him chaining me to the poles.

Somehow, I managed to drop my staff inside the tiny tube. That act alone broke some of the spell as it clattered down inside hollow stone.

Dr. Emp's command still rocked my skull, but I tilted forward, goggles flopping at my neck. Holding my breath against the stench, I began to fall in slowly.

"Stop." His voice was louder now, and I had to obey.

My mind barely registered the tube as I slid. Stone rubbed at my cheeks, but it didn't matter. My body had frozen, as commanded, but gravity let me plummet.

The tube angled, then an opening to my right

clipped my elbow painfully, but I couldn't move. Some distant part knew my face and arms were getting scraped, but I had no thought of reacting. I had ceased to act on my own accord, even my mind seemed locked.

Another angle, another opening, and I slammed the top of my head into Serena's.

"Ow. Get off me."

Her words echoed once in my brain, but I wasn't supposed to do anything. My eyes were open to the pitch black, and I breathed though no words or thoughts formed.

"Tommy. I'm shifting down, be careful of the hole on the side."

Her words bounced about my brain, barely registering. I should have been responding, and I knew it now, but nothing came out.

"Tommy?"

Something wet was on my cheek and my face was beginning to ache. Feeling something was good, right?

There were other voices too, not just Serena. The Oon were below her, whispering. Far above, I could hear someone angry.

A finger poked my eye. "Tommy?"

Where was James? He should have landed on me, as I had on Serena. Blood rushed in my throat. I was sure my face was bleeding. "James," I croaked.

"Did he make it?" Serena asked as pulled her hand away. We were packed in the tube at an angle, head to head. As she shifted down, I slid behind her.

James had heard the same command that I had, except he hadn't followed me. Panic over my friend and the tight confines loosened my muscles so that I pressed out fingers to the walls. I gagged at the reek.

"Down here. Be careful." Ninga was whispering to us, or Serena at least.

"Dr. Emp has James." I stated the obvious, my thoughts still thick, but I could move now.

"We'll get him back." Serena shifted, taking some of the pressure off our heads as I pressed myself in place.

I pivoted in the tube so that I faced the side of the tub, rather than upward, it felt more natural. "How?"

She crawled away. "Careful. Hole on the left. Oh, it is wider down here."

Left meant nothing to me since I couldn't be sure of which way we faced. My fingers, raw from stone on the back sides, helped ease me toward her. The slope was sharp, but not vertical. We did have to go back for James no matter what.

First, we needed to think. If I took off my pack, I wouldn't be as wedged in as I was.

"My staff?" I hoped it hadn't been lost.

"Here." Serena poked my shoulder with the butt of it.

We had a lot to figure out. Getting to James before he was fully controlled was important, but not being caught would matter as well. A hole *was* on my left, but it came in from above. I pressed my hand against something soft and squishy and retreated with a grimace.

There were distant, muffled voices up the shaft.
Vodynash snarls.

They would be searching for us.

"We need a plan," I said.

CHAPTER 21
SOMETHING IN THE PIPES

I EASED myself down a bit more as Serena scraped against stone, maybe clay, deeper below me. Careful not to rub raw skin against the walls, I was pleased to find the dark confines widening quickly.

"I should have stood my ground." Serena's tone was angry.

"Against mind control magic?"

"Earplugs," she replied.

"That we don't have. But – we could make them."

"Exactly." Serena was angry and not too rational.

I could almost sit up.

A voice growled closer to the shaft behind me and I could make out words. "… search outside …" Then they were gone with a snarling reply from a second Vodynash that I couldn't make out. I shivered.

A new opening to my right thwarted my attempt to inch quietly forward and my staff scraped loudly as I slipped.

"Shh." Serena hissed.

"Do you have something to make earplugs with?" I asked.

"Gum. Let me get my backpack off. I've got a flashlight."

I froze as something scratched deep in the pipe to my right. No Vodynash could fit in here. Maybe a rabid, mind controlled Oon? "Did you hear that?"

"No." Serena sounded distracted. "Sen maybe?"

"Where is she?" I spoke quietly, listening.

"She left, hoping Dr. Emp hadn't seen her. I hope he doesn't kill her."

I started to question her about when Sen had left and why he might kill her, then remembered how out of it I'd been from his attempted mind control. The scratch sounded again, almost as if in response to Serena's voice. Maybe it was Sen, clawing her way out. I hoped she'd survive.

If — when we did try to climb back up for James, we'd likely make a lot of noise.

Serena's backpack unzipped, and she grunted in satisfaction before a dull light shone from the depths. It created just enough glow that I could see her and the clay walls of the tube. She sat crouched and her hair was matted as if wet in places. Her eyes flashed toward me and she shook her head. "Headfirst?"

"I fell." About three feet from her, I began twisting my legs up wondering if I could sit as well.

I paused when something knocked on the pipe a few yards behind her. It was a persistent rap that traveled away, as if someone checked for the hollow notes of the clay.

"Vodynash," Ninga whispered. "They know we went in here." I couldn't see her, but she sounded close to Serena.

The knocking stopped and we were all silent. To my right, something skittered in the pipes above. Chills crawled up my neck. I hoped it was Sen escaping.

Serena was staring at my face, wincing. Her hands still dug quietly in her bag. As we waited for the Vodynash to continue their search, hoping they didn't tap on the pipes we sat on, she produced a jar of salve and offered it.

I made as little noise as possible inching toward her and straightening to a crouch in the wider pipe. Surely this was part of the tube we'd seen outside dumping into the pit. If James were with us, I'd suggest we crawl down it and try to escape. The Vodynash were likely waiting there anyway.

After a moment, I took the salve and smeared it on my face, cooling the scrapes. It would help fight infection as well with all this muck on the walls. I wanted to ask if this was where they dumped sewage, but it didn't smell that bad.

"We have to climb back up there," Serena said with her voice barely at a whisper.

"Agreed. Gum?" I was spreading salve on the back of my fingers.

She held up a pack of mint-flavored gum. It was mostly full and frayed from long disuse in her pack. "Last time I had any was a year ago on the flight to

DC. Should work." The scratching in the tube to the side started again and she frowned in silence.

It did sound closer.

We both jumped when knocking sounded much farther down. The rhythm continued for nearly a minute, then something heavy and hard crashed into the pipe. I gritted my teeth, though they were far from us. A second smash cracked clay. The third shattered the pipe.

Muffled Vodynash voices grumbled up the pipe as a distant light flickered on the curved walls far beyond Ninga. The tones hinted at an argument growing down there. The light faded as the yelling grew until I could make out someone calling another "idiot."

Silently, I handed the jar of salve back to Serena. I worked at the straps of my pack, trying to be quiet. My own flashlight was small, but if we were climbing up, I'd like to see what was ahead.

The voices below abruptly faded, leaving us alone again.

"We need a plan," I said with one shoulder free of my straps. In the silence

"Ear plugs and sword," Serena said.

I grimaced. "You'd stab the man?" Maybe his faithful Oon as well.

"For James, yes."

Would I kill someone to save James? I couldn't imagine it. "Maybe just wound him a little and I'll work on getting James out. We'll have to come back down these pipes to escape." That would be more difficult with the broken pipe below us, but they'd moved on.

My heart skipped when someone knocked on the pipe just a yard higher up the tube. I almost shifted in response, but that might have given us away. Heart pounding, I waited for the next rap, wondering if it would be closer or farther. A muffled grumbling sounded outside. I imagined the pipe being cracked open with one of the Vodynash mushroom-head weapons and me plummeting out.

The next knock came farther from me, and I started to breathe again. At some point, they would either have to disassemble the pipe, or believe we'd escaped. Obviously, I hoped the latter.

Two more raps against clay and the Vodynash moved on. I dug in my pack and eventually found the small penlight I carried. If we were going to climb up to save James, we couldn't wait forever.

I flicked on my light, peering up the shaft. My hopes were that they'd moved on from searching the building and were looking outside. Serena's plan of stabbing Dr. Emp might not be necessary if we could just sneak in and free James.

Slowly, I turned around, feet toward Serena. "Are we ready?" I asked, pushing my pack ahead of me.

Neither Serena nor Ninga had answered before furious scratching sounded from the opening beside my legs. Something, some small creature, was coming down to us.

CHAPTER 22
KREMID

NEARLY DROPPING MY PENLIGHT, I twisted trying to shine up into the clay tube. I made it to my side with my staff pinned under me and left elbow tight against the curve above me.

"What —?" Serena leaned on my ankle to shine her light into the opening of the shaft.

Trapped, my chest tightened. "I don't know." It sounded small, not as big as an Oon, but it was certainly getting closer.

I wasn't sure if I should move higher up, or lower, closer to Serena. Wriggling, I tried to free my staff. Even if I just intended to use it as a clumsy club, I'd rather have it between me and the critter.

"It's —" Serena shifted higher on my leg, Athame darting for the opening.

A lizard head, bearded like a South Florida iguana, darted out of the pipe and snapped at my flashlight.

"Jeez." My light was knocked loose and I yanked

my hand back. The size of a cat, but with a short neck and stubby front claws, the creature had teeth the size of my own. Clumsily, I tried to shove my staff, still wedged under my knee, at it.

The lizard pulled back eying my hand that I'd mistakenly pulled up toward my face. Serena pressed against my legs as she lunged, trying to stab it, but her reach wasn't long enough. It was enough to distract the thick head though. The eyes were huge and round, the size of my thumb.

When it twisted to face her, long claws braced on my staff. I had hold of my focal, that was all I needed to cast magic. It didn't have to point, my focus did.

The oversized lizard pivoted to center on Serena's blade and a thick hind leg emerged from the hole to give it leverage. The skin was gray scales. Its tail bent back into the opening.

Serena was still stabbing at it though she couldn't get close enough being wedged against my boots.

Its back leg shifted forward, and I could see it lunging for her hand and even face. "Careful." I took a deep breath, focusing a slowing spell.

When she stuck her blade forward, the lizard jerked and clawed my pants as it snapped at Serena's hand. Metal made a dull scrape against scales and the creature whipped its teeth away as if trying to rip her skin. Her flashlight still shone at the creature, and blood welled on her knuckle.

"Sebis Halaal." I cast the slowing spell at the creature.

Its head tilted up, eye rolling to see me over its

shoulder. The movement was more languid than its earlier snapping attacks.

Serena, despite the blood on her hand, stuck her blade deep in the lizard's mouth.

"Kora Beeh," Serena nearly yelled the slashing spell in our tight confines. As she called out her magic, the creature split open with a spray of gore, and I closed my eyes. Liquid, blood or worse, splattered against my face.

I whisked it off with a shiver and found the lizard's head torn in half back to its shoulder, exactly as I'd imagined it. It was dead.

"What was that?" Gingerly, I shoved the remains back toward the opening it had come down.

"A Kremid." Ninga's voice quavered from beyond Serena.

Serena was mumbling and shifting off my legs to get room to remove her pack. Her right hand had a large gash atop the knuckle nearly up to her thumb. "Venomous?"

"I don't know. We stay away from them."

That sounded like a good plan. "What do you think it was doing down here?" I retrieved my penlight and double-checked the deadness of the creature.

"They live in underground tunnels."

We weren't underground, though it felt like it. I guessed we were somewhere between the third and second level, or perhaps down as far as just above the first. Had the Vodynash tossed it in here to mess with us?

Opening her pack Serena juggled blade, flashlight, and the jar of salve we'd luckily brought. "Are you all right?" I asked her.

"Yeah. Flesh wound." She flexed her hand to prove it.

While she tended to her wound, I shifted and eased my staff free. My spell had worked enough for her to stab it and finish it off with her own magic. It could have gone much worse. It felt like hours that we'd been down here. While I waited for Serena, I retrieved the gum she'd given me and began chewing it. The minty flavor just reminded me of how much it stunk in the pipes.

"Ready," she said from behind.

I began inching forward, nudging my loose pack ahead and scanning with my penlight. When we reached an opening, I paused to listen, but nothing scratched inside.

Each shift I made sounded loud against the clay. If the Vodynash sat patiently waiting, we would have been easy to hear.

As the slant steepened, the tube grew tighter and I spotted where I slid uncontrolled leaving a scrape along the sides. The salve had made my face feel better, hopefully I wouldn't appear too bad. The thought of my mom remarking on it reminded me of the portal we couldn't pass through. I'd relied on finding Miss Fitz to lead us through, but all we'd accomplished was finding the Dewi Sri — and getting James caught. We weren't doing very well.

If we could free James and escape, we'd be in

better shape. My heart sank, not believing it was actually possible. We were up against a building of Vodynash and Dr. Emp's mind control. He might have other magic as well. A chill ran up my spine, imagining us all like the drab who'd been collecting water outside. Never finding Miss Fitz. Never getting home. I couldn't leave James, but I had little hope.

We had to be getting close to the top of the waste chute on the fourth floor. That just made my chest tighten.

CHAPTER 23
JAMES

I HAD to keep my heels and knees pinning me against the walls near the top as the shaft turned vertical. Serena didn't say a word as I stopped and listened before inching higher and pausing again. I doubted any of us wanted to play whack-a-mole with the Vodynash.

There were no voices or snarls above though, even when it became light enough that I turned off and pocketed my light. The gum had lost all its flavor and I didn't look forward to using if for earplugs. Neither did I want to end up captured with James.

I let my pack shift down beside my head when I reached the top and peered over the edge. They'd left the door open and I could see to the wall that wrapped around the stairwell. Legs aching, I waited for a long moment, listening.

Taking a deep breath, I shifted up a few times, then put my pack on the floor and drew my staff out and braced on the outer rim. The dark room had a few baskets lining the outer corners. I had a good view out the door and still there wasn't a sound.

"It might be clear," I whispered down into the tube.

Pinning myself with one knee and heel, I drew out a leg and balanced on the edge before standing. Staff ready, I crept to the door, glancing one way then the other, half expecting to see Dr. Emp and little Wukad waiting for me.

I was peeking around the corner by the time Serena exited the tube. "Anything?" she asked.

Tilting farther out, I studied the edge of the stage and the stairs winding up. "No. Isn't that odd?"

"Yes. We just need to be careful and smart."

I blinked when I realized Serena still held some hope. Though, our magic had worked against the Kremid. My jaw tightened and I straightened. "Careful and smart," I agreed. My magic wasn't all that useless. My push and slow spells were my strongest, I needed to rely on them.

As Ninga climbed out of the waste chute, I motioned for her to wait with my pack. "In case we need to leave in a hurry." She didn't need to take any risks.

Leaning forward, I found James. He was manacled to a pole nearly facing us. His pack was open and discarded at the foot of the stage. Peeking out at the rest of the room, I didn't find Dr. Emp or any of his minions. I raised my staff at my friend, but his eyes were dull and focused on the space in front of him.

"You keep watch, I'll free James," I said.

"Plugs," suggested Serena.

I pulled out the gum, splitting the pale wad into two sections, then shoved the nastiness into my ears. The whoosh of my pulse took away any sound. Stepping out from the doorway, I swiveled my head, still searching for a trap.

James never shifted as I approached. The other Oon we'd seen earlier still sat where he had, arms pinned above his head as he stared at a far wall. How long did it take for Dr. Emp to properly condition someone? My friend hadn't been here that long.

My eyes flitted from his dull stare to the top of the winding staircase where I expected to see Wukad watching me through the railing, but we were alone. The Vodynash might have given up searching inside and were scouring the dunes by now. Would Dr. Emp have joined them, or was he upstairs?

I couldn't hear my feet across the wood, so I crept more carefully than I might otherwise. Serena followed me a couple paces but held back with her eyes blazing intensely.

They'd let James keep his gadget belt and pocketed vest. His arms rested wide with the manacles holding his wrists barely a foot over his head.

After all my apprehension, it seemed too easy as I padded to the stage, then eased myself up. No one stood visible on the floor above the circular staircase. I was tempted to take out my gooey earplugs, just to check if there were voices up there. Something herbal and sweet wafted in the air near the shelves, but I ignored it.

James didn't turn to me when I slipped to his side. I hoped I wouldn't have to slide him off the stage. Dr. Emp's effect had worn off with me, but I'd hardly gotten the brunt of it.

The manacles were held on with a simple threaded bolt and nut that I expected would be tight, but they unscrewed easily. If Dr. Emp's victims weren't already stunned, they'd easily free themselves. I grinned as the manacle loosened and James's hand flopped loose, dropping to his side. I felt the thud and grimaced, glancing up.

In my mind, I saw, or imagined, what would happen next. James's face turning to me, raising his wand, and speaking a spell I couldn't hear; then being stunned to my knees, and Dr. Emp's feet on the staircase. Hands frozen in the air, I snapped my eyes to James. It couldn't happen that way.

Somehow, I was sure it would.

I stepped my left foot back, and James's face tightened from the flaccid, vacant stare. His free hand moved for his belt where he kept his telescoping wand.

This was a trap. Dr. Emp had already turned James against us. We couldn't save him.

My right foot retreated, and I focused on my staff. "Sebis Halaal." The slow spell rung oddly in my skull with my ears plugged.

It hit James though and his motion slowed as he reached for his wand.

I had to run. "Trap," I yelled to Serena as I spun away.

She frowned, unable to hear me, but watching the strange interaction between me and our friend. Both of her blades were out. Her only movement was to take a step toward us. Serena needed to run.

Rolling off the edge of the stage, I felt the dullness of a stun spell graze across me. I hit the floor face-first, barely understanding what had happened. As I rolled, I caught Dr. Emp's boots at the top of the stairs and stomping down.

With what thought I could muster, I jabbed my staff in James's direction and hit him again with another slow spell. I would have used stun myself, but it was the worst spell in my arsenal.

James stood now, one hand brandishing his wand, and the other still caught in the manacle he strained against. My second attack had a better impact than the first, and his lips hung parted open as if unable to complete his words.

Serena's stun spell was as weak as mine, but together we might be able to silence James enough to drag him away. Unfortunately, Dr. Emp was barreling down the stairs with his Oon, Wukad. We didn't have time.

The hairs on my neck prickled, and I could see Serena attacked by two Vodynash. Spinning, I faced her.

There was one, lurching around the corner of the staircase. My yelling and spellcasting hadn't been quiet.

We were pinned, with the only escape back to Ninga and the waste chute. I started running in that direction, and from one of the small wardrobes near it another Vodynash jumped out and raced toward us.

Serena saw my shocked pause, and turned to eye both Vodynash, her stance adjusting for battle.

We had James with his stun spell, one of his best. Dr. Emp and Wukad with whatever they could do. Worst, we had the brutish Vodynash that we'd done everything we could to avoid.

That left Serena and her swords to fight — and me; just an average witch.

We were trapped. I would have to fight. My magic would have to work.

CHAPTER 24
THIRD OPTION

I DASHED to join Serena as the two Vodynash raced toward her, the closest target. My top spell was push, but that hardly nudged back Chet, and the creatures easily outweighed him.

They both had their gray clubs with their strange mushroom heads. The one who had been hiding in the stairwell was the nearest and I slid beside Serena with staff raised. It wore what appeared to be a too wide smile, but the small eyes glared at us. Its shaggy fur shook with each stride.

"Xaban Sait." My push spell shifted the Vodynash's step enough to cause it to stumble.

Serena used the creature's awkward move to jump to the side and forced it further off balance by jabbing at it. She sliced at its feet, not appearing to actually intend a hit, but forcing it to swing too soon with the club.

"Sebis Halaal." Stepping back with her, I

slammed a slow spell into the Vodynash and it worked.

The Vodynash pivoted awkwardly into the path of the second of its kind, just arriving to our battle.

After another feint with her sword, Serena jabbed her Athame at it and spoke the same slash spell she'd used on the lizard. "Kora Beeh." The damage was disappointing as the creature's fur ruffled and it opened its mouth wide in a silent howl before lunging at her.

I imagined the Vodynash backhand Serena, just as she began a low strike toward its legs. Instinctively, I jabbed the garnet of my staff at its face, surprising it just enough to distract it.

She landed a quick jab, metal tip of the sword sinking into fur, and darted back just as the backhand started. Sharp nails whizzed past her face but missed.

We both leaped a yard back when the club of the second Vodynash slammed into the floor at our feet.

Dr. Emp was speaking only a few yards behind us, and I was very grateful for the sticky gum in my ears. Aiming at both of the Vodynash, I released another slowing spell. The first had matted wet fur, leaking something grayish rather than dark red blood, from Serena's attacks, but it barely bled and without it showing any sign of feeling the pain.

I might just die here. The thought freed me somewhat and I slammed another slowing spell at the pair, giving Serena a chance to score three more stabs before they forced us back toward Dr. Emp and Wukad. They stood there watching.

Dr. Emp's expression was wrinkled with frustration. His words had no effect on us. His left hand he'd tucked in his long, outlandish jacket's pocket while his right tugged at his collar — no, he touched the chain holding the eyeball around his neck. There was another odd piece of jewelry dangling with the sphere of glass; a dull metal hand that clasped an upraised mallet hung just behind the shiny eye.

James, visible just beyond the wide brim of Dr. Emp's zany hat, had turned to work on his other manacle. If — when he freed himself, he might get close enough to stun us. My chest tightened at the thought of what else he might throw at us.

I lashed out again against the Vodynash with slow and push spells, but though they now had multiple wet patches in their fur, they weren't relenting. Again, I saw a devastating blow against Serena before it happened, and feigned a jab with the point of my staff to distract the Vodynash before it swung the deadly weapon.

She dodged out of the way, bringing us another pace closer to Dr. Emp. Hair clung to her forehead with sweat and she had to swipe it out of her eyes.

The skirmish had barely lasted a minute, but I wasn't too shocked to see a third Vodynash turn the corner from the stairwell. With all the noise I couldn't hear, we'd have every Vodynash up on the fourth floor with us — maybe a few Oons as well.

We might die here, and my heart raced like I knew it, but I wasn't giving up any more than Serena was. I tried one of my lesser effective spells, explode.

"Shabla-dain." The fur on the Vodynash ruffled, but nothing exploded. The creature's eyes did squint in certain hate though.

When Serena threw a fireball nearly point blank against the Vodynash with the most wounds, I thought we might have some hope. Flames burst against fur, widening the creature's eyes. The fire wisped into smoke leaving a blackened section on his shoulder and a reek in the air.

I saw the backhand coming at her in my mind before it happened, but when I spoke a push spell while jamming my staff at the nose of the Vodynash, it slapped it away. Then it hit Serena.

The blow made my teeth clench as she was lifted off her feet from the impact. Her Athame toppled from her hand. She hit the ground two paces to my right and skidded on her back. Her sword spun even farther.

Two of the Vodynash spun to follow her, while the one who'd just knocked her away was about to swing his club at my head. I saw it clearly in my mind and dipped under it. The breeze ruffled my hair.

"Xaban Siat." I pushed him back and slung a spell at the closest creature bearing down on Serena. "Sebis Halaal." The slowing spell worked enough as she scrambled to get to her feet before it reached her.

My Vodynash twisted to bring its club low and up into me, but I saw it in my mind, and pivoted in time.

I touched my staff to the side of his face. "Kora Beeh." The slash spell wet his temple and he jerked away from me, wide mouth showing low teeth. He hadn't liked that.

Serena had skittered clear of her pursuers, picking up her sword, though her Athame was behind her attackers. I was too far and partially blocked from helping her. They'd separated us, and there would be more coming I bet.

Seeing where my Vodynash would strike next, I dodged and blasted spells at it, but I'd been pushed back to within a couple paces of Dr. Emp and his Oon.

My next vision surprised me with two layers. The first was the Vodynash shoving me backward, where Dr. Emp stabbed me in the back with a short, black-bladed knife. The second was of me pivoting to miss the shove, and getting stabbed in the side.

I needed a third option.

Serena was dancing between two Vodynash, cutting her way free.

Wide-eyed Ninga peered around the corner of the doorway to the waste chute.

James had just hopped off the stage and was stalking toward us.

I spun, facing Dr. Emp. His right hand still touched the chain at his neck, but he held a very ugly knife at his left side, the black tip pointed toward my stomach. The weapon seemed to drink light. His Oon, Wukad, wore an evil grin, for a rabbit.

The slam of the Vodynash's fist between my shoulders took all my air out of my lungs. The impact propelled me forward. Now, I saw a vision of the dark blade stabbing deep into my gut and knew my skin would begin to turn as pitch black as the blade was. It was an evil magic. I would die, Serena would follow, and James would be trapped forever.

I shoved my staff forward as I launched toward the tall man. My only focus was his blade. The old white wood of my focal slapped against the black metal before he started to thrust.

Dr. Emp fumbled slightly, jarred by the move.

My head bounced off his chest from the momentum provided by the Vodynash punch. "Sebis Halaal." My slow spell worked as Dr. Emp barely shifted. It gave me the opportunity to push aside the black knife.

Then my next vision came.

The Vodynash would swing his club into my right side, breaking my arm that held the staff keeping the blade away. I had little doubt what would happen after that.

Dr. Emp's eyes were wide at me being so close — and not skewered on his blade. He clutched at his chain, as if it were dear to him. How dear? The chain, or the odd jewelry hanging from it?

I had less than a second to act before my vision of a broken arm came true.

Teeth grinding, I grabbed Dr. Emp's eyeball and hammer pieces — and yanked.

The creature's club smashed into my upper arm, just a couple inches above the elbow. I felt the crack, since I couldn't hear it. Pain shrieked through my entire arm, and I my scream echoed in my bones. My whole body flew to the side and I toppled to the floor. My staff bounced at my feet.

Agony followed my every move, welling tears in my eyes. When I skidded to land on my left hip and shoulder, my vision dimmed as my right arm flopped off my hip. Bones grated.

I clenched the odd jewelry in my left fist. The chain glittered as it slid away across the floor.

At first, Dr. Emp took a step toward me, as if to retrieve his glass eyeball and metal hammer, or stab me, or both. Then he froze, gawking at the Vodynash in front of him. The creature was no longer interested in me and seemed to be preparing to club his master instead.

Dr. Emp shoved the evil blade into the Vodynash, gave one glare to me, then raced for the stairs, leaving Wukad behind. The Oon appeared shocked at first, then yipped and darted to follow with a raging pair of Vodynash close on his furry heels. The dying creature kept touching the blade as it dropped to its knees then collapsed.

I nearly fainted from pain when I rolled to see Serena free of her attackers and watching them with bewilderment.

James stood five paces away with a far more befuddled expression than hers on his face as he stared at his wand in his hand, then us.

I opened my hand and peered at the two items. They were talismans of magic somehow. I'd stolen Dr. Emp's magic. It was the only reason why the Vodynash were attacking him, not us, and why

James was confused — and not slinging spells at me.

We still needed to get out of the castle. The Vodynash might not be under Dr. Emp's control anymore, but I didn't think they were very nice on their own.

"Grab your pack, make for the waste chute," I called out to James.

He stiffened, then turned briskly to comply.

"Damn." I was holding the talismans, and I guessed one of them forced people to do what I said. I held my breath as I pushed to my knee, right arm swinging with a jolt of agony. The room dimmed again.

Serena was at my side, sheathing her sword and helping me up. She winced at the sight of my limp arm.

With my good hand, I shoved the jewelry into my pocket, hoping that would dull their magic. I didn't need everyone doing whatever I said.

Serena handed me my staff and we both watched James marching toward the door to the chute with his pack. She shrugged questioningly, and I rolled my eyes. Explanations could come once we were clear of the present danger.

Cringing at every step, I strode toward the chute while Serena retrieved her Athame and followed.

On the stage, I could make out the one Oon working at their manacle and freeing themselves. I had forgotten about them.

We'd survived and rescued James. I'd learned some weird new stuff that helped me fight, and that my magic was better than I thought. As a bonus, Dr. Emp was running from his Vodynash. I'd expected worse.

James and Ninga waited by the chute. He wore a blank, but attentive expression. I really hoped the mind control would wear off. Until I was sure that deep in my pocket they'd have no effect, I'd keep my mouth shut.

I didn't relish sliding down the tubes with a broken arm, but it was time to leave.

CHAPTER 25
FINDING MISS FITZ

I WAS at the door to the waste chute when another Vodynash dashed out of the stairwell. Leaning on my staff more than holding it, I sagged. Indiana Jones might have found this kind of stuff fun, but exhaustion took all the excitement from it.

The creature's head snapped toward the circular stair and the rooms above, then raced there instead of toward us.

Balancing my staff in the crook of my elbow, I plucked a wad of gum out of my ears. I could hear Dr. Emp yelling in the distance. I cleared out my other ear, wincing at the movement. I really didn't want to slide down the tube, but we couldn't risk meeting a Vodynash climbing down the stairs.

Serena was digging in her pack with one hand and plucking gum out with the other. "Need to get you in a sling. Is the humerus broken? It looks like it."

My skin was swelling like I had Chet's muscles — well, not exactly. "Yeah, I'm pretty sure."

"Then this will hurt." She dug with both hands now.

James stood examining his wand with a frown. Ninga had climbed to the edge of the tube, rabbit legs dangling over.

"Are you okay, James?" I figured compelling him to answer that wouldn't be bad, if the magic was still active in my pocket.

He blinked, then shook his head. "I guess so. My thoughts are foggy. I remember …" Shivering, he slid his wand down and tucked it in his belt. "I'm sorry. Really. I'm sorry."

I shook my head and regretted the motion. My shoulder and neck were on fire while I wasn't sure I could feel my fingers. My mom was going to freak. A cold chill spread over my chest. We still had no sure way back.

Serena produced a roll of gauze. "It's thin, so we'll have to do a bunch of wraps. I'm going to move your lower arm, and it's going to hurt. Maybe bite down on your staff."

I huffed. "I'll survive. We should hurry."

She loosened a long length of the white gauze. I nearly fainted when she moved me. My teeth hurt as she wrapped cloth around my forearm. "You were pretty amazing up there."

My eyebrows already climbing up my forehead, I just blinked. "What?"

"How did you move like that? Dodging their swings?" With my hand pulled up to my chest, she looped gauze around the back of my neck and back down.

Releasing my clenched jaw, I tried to explain. "I could just see it before it happened. I'd get this image of where they'd hit me, then make sure I wasn't there."

James slid on his pack and nodded. "Second sight. A rare thing."

I remembered the conversation Miss Fitz had with my parents. She'd said those same words. *So this was the danger?* She'd promised to be there to protect me — us. Had she lied to my parents? We could have died.

Serena scoffed, looping about my arm then about my neck again. "Might have wanted to dodge this hit. It is going to take a long time to heal. My brother broke his arm."

My choice hadn't been better. That blade had been the only thing to kill a Vodynash.

James had a headlamp out and lit it, peering down into the clay tube. "What's down here?"

"Hopefully a way out," said Serena. She tied off a knot at my neck, and cut the excess with her Athame. "We've got the Dewi Sri. Now we need to find Miss Fitz. Let's go. I'll follow last."

Ninga dropped down with her hands out against the walls.

James sighed, strapped the headlamp around his

neck, and stepped over the edge. He grunted as he slid down.

Serena nudged her chin toward the pipe. "Be careful." She took my staff and pack in one hand.

I smiled. "I think I know where Miss Fitz is."

She frowned as I shifted my legs into the tube and lowered inside with one hand. "Where?"

Without answering, I tried to climb down by pinning heel and knee, but slipped. My forehead scraped clay, then my shoulder bumped the side and the fiery agony returned full force. Tears in my eyes and gritting teeth, I slid down the stinky tube.

Eventually, I slowed and caught myself with my heels. "James?" There was a faint glow from his headlamp. My light was in my pack's pocket.

"Yeah?"

"Just checking." I guessed by the angle we weren't down as far as we'd been before.

Serena's light flicked on above me. "Are we moving?"

I inched down, cringing. "Yep."

It was a few minutes before we reached where the Vodynash had smashed open the pipe. An entire section angling across an empty room was gone with no way to climb across. When I arrived, James helped me down.

The castle was quiet. "What floor?" I asked James.

"Ninga thinks it's the second. We'll have to use the stairs, but she's scouting now. I believe all the Oon have left."

My arm felt numb if I didn't bump it. The ache was there and it had swelled. "If they were all freed, like you and the Vodynash, it would make sense."

Serena handed my staff to me and tossed my pack to James. "Do we take the front path, or through the dunes again?"

I smiled. "Let's ask Ninga."

Our Oon escort appeared as we peeked out of the door flap into a hall with familiar rough-hewn walls. The air smelled almost pleasant after the tubes. "Stairs are clear."

Making sure to follow just behind her, I spoke casually. "So, still no sign of Miss Fitz?" I asked her.

Ninga was quiet as she brought us into the now empty Vodynash barracks. "Nope."

"Because there's no mirrors?" I asked with slight sarcasm. If I was right, she had to admit it. I doubted I was wrong. She'd stuck by us the entire time.

She stopped at the landing before the stairwell and turned to study me. "Clever boy."

I swore, and Serena gasped as Ninga — Miss Fitz, trotted down the stairs. The Oon began to grow with each step. The fur on her head frizzed out into white hair while the rest grew into her black turtleneck and sensible slacks. Shoes clacked on stone.

"You let us nearly die," Serena said from behind.

"Baugh, you were handling the situation just fine." Ninga's high-pitched young voice was gone and Miss Fitz waved a dismissive hand in the air.

"I was a zombie," said James.

"Technically a thrall," Miss Fitz replied.

We were at the front doors and both were open. "So, this was what my parents were worried about?" I asked.

She peered over the rim of her glasses. "Eavesdropping is bad manners." Miss Fitz took a moment for me to squirm, then led us outside onto the stone flats. "We learned what we needed to. You've got the gene for second sight. They'll be happy."

My eyes went cross-eyed when I foolishly tried to raise my arm. "Mom's not going to be happy about a broken arm."

"We'll fix it before you get home. Mostly." Miss Fitz started at a brisk walk.

The gray domain stretched out ahead of us with a line of the forest and mountains behind them. I didn't see any Oon or Vodynash running about.

"The Oon are okay?" I asked Miss Fitz. "Free?"

"Should be. I hadn't expected that, but it was a pleasant surprise. They won't have to worry about Dr. Emp."

What had she expected? "The Vodynash?"

"They will probably head back to the mountains where they come from. I hope." Miss Fitz glanced back at us. "Drink up. You've got a long walk ahead."

James had a light smile on his face as he kept up on my other side.

Serena was scowling beside me. "I'm still mad."

"I'd think you would be proud of Tommy. He's passed a valuable test to come into his birthright and learned a little confidence."

"It wasn't nice of you."

"Tommy wouldn't have learned if he expected me to drag his bacon off the fire. He's becoming a fine witch. Besides, *you* got to kill a Taar. Nasty creatures who hunt the Oon. I thought you liked to stab things." Miss Fitz sounded amused, then her face tightened with her more common stern expression. "I will want my sword put back, by the way."

Serena rolled her eyes, but a smile flicked over her face. "I'll put it back."

"We can get through the portal now?" It was a dumb question, but I asked.

"With me. You can get through as well now, with the eye of Badu. That one you can keep as a souvenir. The hammer of Tarim gets locked away." As she mentioned it, I reached down, but she shook her head. "Keep it safe in your pocket until we get back to the classroom."

It was a nasty talisman, not that I knew about many. The eye of Badu sounded cool, and I got to keep it. "So, I can go to other domains and realms?"

"You'll want to hold onto that until you learn a little more. The Neverdoor is still a no."

"How did you know we'd go through this time?"

She scoffed and raised her wrist, as if missing the bracelet. "I knew you wouldn't be able to resist following Dr. Emp."

I frowned. We wouldn't have gone through if we hadn't seen Dr. Emp, but that was just simple luck and timing. "How did you know we'd see him?"

"Shh. Secrets. Learn and find out."

James handed me the water bottle from my pack. I sipped at it. *Was there some magic she'd used, or had sprung a trap on all of us?*

Either way, we were on our way home, and I was starving.

CHAPTER 26
ELECTRICITY

TWO DAYS later I sat on the floor of our tree house playing a game against Serena with a stiff but usable right hand. Miss Fitz's healing magic had been uncomfortable, but not as painful as I'd feared.

"You are going to die," Serena growled.

I pursed my lips and fought to outmaneuver her. The memories of our excursion into the Gray Domain had haunted my sleep.

James smiled, working on one of his tablets. "Three, two, one."

The light hanging from the ceiling glowed into life. He'd gotten the turbine working without climbing outside. His drone dropped to the roof with a metallic thud.

"Cool." I winced as Serena killed me. "Electricity."

She smiled and rested a controller on her leg. "Very cool."

Skittering noises sounded as James ambled

toward the window. "I should have built this before. It's better than climbing that ladder. I'm not sure it would have worked for the whole project though." Reaching up, he retrieved his new bot, a metallic box with six legs, one of which were a Phillips-head screwdriver and the other a socket wrench. His eyes were dark. He wasn't sleeping well either. "We've got class in an hour."

Serena raised her controller with a questioning eyebrow. "Ready?"

I sighed and nodded. My game was off, and she knew it, but it felt better to play than sitting around distracted. The trip to the Gray Domain had changed us all. I still wanted to believe I was average, but we'd been through some amazing things. I'd not only survived, but done well. The Oon were free from Dr. Emp, and even Miss Fitz hadn't thought we'd do that.

Too bad second sight didn't work with video games.

The ride to the library was hot and sweaty. My right arm worked fine, but there was a dull ache when I used it. Miss Fitz said I could use it to tell when it was going to rain, and I hoped she'd been joking.

"What did they think?" asked James, yelling over the light whine of his bike.

"Who?" *About what?*

"Your parents."

Oh, the second sight. "They were happy." In truth, Mom seemed like she'd been worried she'd never see me again. Had Miss Fitz ever lost anyone on these tests?

"I bet." He'd been quiet about his parents.

"How about yours?"

"Erm, I think my mother is upset with Miss Fitz, even when I told her that she'd been there the whole time as Ninga."

"Yeah, that hadn't made my mom happy either." My dad had been more interested in the details. Mom had made mac and cheese though so I knew she felt bad about my broken arm.

Serena's hair whipped as she spoke from ahead of us. "Mom says the Vodynash aren't originally from the Gray Domain."

"What did she think about you fighting them?" I asked. My mom had been slightly horrified that we'd been using our slash spell on them.

"She said to go for the tendons in the back of the leg next time."

We had very different moms.

The library was wonderfully cool when we walked in, and nearly deserted. Our portal at the end of the hall was clear and Serena stepped through first, leaving me and James keeping watch.

When I stepped out onto the winding staircase, the metal grate reminded me of Dr. Emp's steps.

Miss Fitz waited at her desk for us while the older class finished up at the lab. We hadn't seen her since we'd returned and she'd healed my arm. The Never-door was closed at the far end of the room and the Dewi Sri was back on its shelf opposite her.

The scent of cinnamon wafted through the air. James followed me down the stairs.

"Do you think they killed Dr. Emp; the Vodynash that is?" The question had been haunting me.

"He's a bit too tricky for that. No magic of his own, but he hoards talismans. We don't have to worry about him, since he doesn't have the eye of Badu."

I touched the bulge of the glass eyeball hanging deep under my shirt. "I didn't mean I wanted him dead." Even the dead Vodynash had haunted my dreams.

She nodded thoughtfully and rose from her chair. "I'd put money on him surviving. I'll let you know next time I visit." With a brisk gesture, she motioned us toward our seats.

The other Oon had known Ninga, so Miss Fitz must have been there before as her. Why?

"Shields?" Serena asked.

Miss Fitz strode ahead of us. "Yes. Now you can imagine how useful they'd be."

I headed for my notebook, checking on the older group rinsing out glass measuring cups and equipment. Vic nodded when he saw me, but I doubt he knew what we'd gone through. Someday, when the other older kids weren't around, I'd see if he'd had similar tests at my age.

Chet spoke loudly to Piper working with him at the sink. "What a wonderfully hot day to enjoy with friends at my pool. Everyone will be there, enjoying their afternoon while you losers trudge around on your little bicycles."

"It's going to be a fantastic party, Chet." Piper was playing it up with him as she normally did when he teased us.

I took my seat close to the front and leaned forward in case they tried the stink trick when they left. Glass rattled in the lab as they put the last bits away.

Miss Fitz began writing spells on the board with a sigil beside each. I did want to learn shields more now than two days ago. She was right.

The bowl of berries that I'd left on the lab table that morning was empty. Chet raised his eyebrows when I glanced at it. "Sorry, forgot to leave you any."

Miss Fitz chuckled. Chet was grinning with purple teeth.

"Have fun at the pool," I said to him.

AFTERWORD

I'm thrilled you made it here to the end !

A quick thanks and a hope that you enjoyed this story, if you did then a review is always helpful.

Contact us at Inkd Pub if you'd like to join the ARC team or Beta readers. support@inkdpub.com

ALSO BY KEVIN A DAVIS

Please head to my website and join my mailing list if you'd like to be kept up to date on this series or my other books.

DRC Files - An episodic paranormal procedural series - ages 13+

Book One: Atlanta's Guide to Cryptids

Book Two: Tallahassee's Manual on Arcane Artifacts

Book Three: Carolina's Handbook on Summoning

Book Four: New Orleans Register of Vampires

Khimmer Chronicles - contemporary fantasy with magic and cryptids in modern day Tallahassee, Florida - ages 15+

"A plucky protagonist who's still finding her way propels this fantasy adventure." Kirkus

https://www.kirkusreviews.com/book-reviews/kevin-a-davis/wights-wrath/

Wight's Wrath - Book One

Death's Contract - Book Two

Fate's Betrayal - Book Three

High Fae's Quest - Book Four

Friday's Fifth - Book Five

Nyx's Blade - The Origin Story

AngelSong Series - contemporary fantasy with fallen angels and angels in modern day Eugene, Oregon - ages 14+

Penumbra - Book One

Red Tempest - Book Two

Coerced - Book Three

Demons' Lair - Book Four

Infrared - Book Five

If you haven't read the Origin story of the **AngelSong** series, *Shattered Blood*, then download a free ebook or purchase the paperback or audible on Amazon.

Find out more

Website KevinArthurDavis.com

Facebook @KevinArthurDavis

KevinADavis on Instagram

KevinADavisUF on Twitter

ACKNOWLEDGMENTS

I'm glad that April enjoyed my foray into middle-grade since her editing and proofing has made the story shine. Since the beginning, she's given me nothing but encouragement on my writing. If you're looking forward to the next one, you have her to thank.

A. Balsamo (April), my editor, works her own magic with insightful development and copyedit. If you enjoy this story, it's largely due to her.

The Fireside Group; Tim, Siena, Rosemary, Mark, Vail, Billy, and Katharine challenge me to do better and let me brainstorm a lot of what I'm working on with them. Arrash and Michele from Jody Lynn Nye's DragonCon workshop keep me on task with the most intricate details and loving support. Dianne and Brett from Apex have been there for me.

I still miss David Farland's loving guidance. Please pick up one of his books and enjoy the magical words he endowed upon the world. Writers, study his lessons at Apex Writers.

Jody Lynn Nye's Dragoncon workshop will always be my go to suggestion for an in-person critique for any aspiring writers. Her insight is invaluable.

Another suggestion for new and developing writers is the Authors Workshop Track at JordanCon where guests, including writers, editors, and publishers, work with authors directly. I'm biased about this track.

Heather Norris and Benson Strickland have supported me so much with this series and more that they deserve a big Thanks as well.

Thank you, dear reader, for listening to my tales.

ALSO BY INKD PUB

Speculative Fiction - fantasy and sci-fi

Hidden Villains

Hidden Villains: Arise

Hidden Villains: Betrayed

Our Horror anthology

Behind the Shadows

Behind the Shadows II

Our Spooky anthology

Noncorporeal

Noncorporeal II

Mystery

Detectives, Sleuths, & Nosy Neighbors

Please visit us at InkdPub.com or Facebook.

www.ingramcontent.com/pod-product-compliance
Lightning Source LLC
Chambersburg PA
CBHW011430310726
48972CB00011B/3003